Disaster Aboard the "Regina"

Pam's lips parted as she stared at Geneva, trying to see what she was doing.

The other girl was burning something that looked to Pam like a letter. She held it above an ash tray and the light from the flame gave her intent face an eerie unreality. Pam was appalled to see how close the fire licked to Geneva's flimsy voluminous costume.

The quick shocked intake of Pam's breath sounded loud at such close range. Geneva whirled around in surprise and, as she did so, the burning paper dropped from her fingers. A gasping scream escaped her as the wide flare of her skirt caught fire before Pam's horrified eyes . . .

SHOWBOAT
SUMMER

Rosamond du Jardin

A BERKLEY HIGHLAND BOOK
published by
BERKLEY PUBLISHING CORPORATION

To Professor W. D. Mitchell and the
Hiram College Showboat troupe, who
generously helped me secure the authentic background material on which
this fictional story is based.

Published by arrangement with
J. B. Lippincott Company

BERKLEY HIGHLAND EDITION, MAY, 1964

BERKLEY HIGHLAND BOOKS are published by
Berkley Publishing Corporation,
15 East 26th Street, New York, N. Y. 10010

Printed in the United States of America

CONTENTS

1	Arrival	7
2	Welcome to the *Regina*	13
3	Meeting	20
4	Two Days Till Opening	27
5	A Break for Pam	34
6	Buff Makes a Decision	42
7	Opening Night	45
8	A Surprise for Pam	52
9	A Quarrel and a Question	59
10	Feud	67
11	Scene in a Post Office	74
12	Bad News	81
13	Visitors from Home	89
14	Buff Takes a Hand	96
15	Trouble for Jeff	103
16	A Sad Trip	109
17	Penny's and Mike's Surprise	116
18	A Special Opening Night	124
19	Near Disaster	130
20	The Show Goes On	137

CHAPTER ONE

ARRIVAL

The beaten-up old station wagon, with Hardwood College lettered across the door, lumbered down the street that sloped so steeply toward the riverbank. It swung into the empty graveled parking lot and Mike Bradley, his b nd head bare and his blue eyes glinting with enthusiasm, braked it to a halt and announced, pointing, "There she 's, the *Regina* herself, last traveling showboat on the rivers. Isn't she something? Didn't I tell you?"

Pam and Penny Howard, on the seat beside him, stared wordlessly for a moment at the scene framed by the windshield. The river stretched broad and greenish-blue in the bright afternoon sunshine, edged with the dusty green of straggly trees and shrubbery and the mellowed contrasting hues of old water-front buildings. Off in the distance the high span of a long bridge arched gracefully against the clear blue sky. But all this was only background for the double-decked, white-painted craft that rode proudly on the water and at which the twins were staring in thrilled wonder. There were touches of green trimming on pilothouse and superstructure. Huge green letters all along one side of the vessel read *SHOWBOAT* atop the pilothouse to the fore and aft decks, imparting a very gala air. Straight out of a Mark Twain novel the whole picture seemed. Ladies in hoopskirts and gentlemen with sideburns and tall beaver hats would have appeared quite in keeping, alighting from horsedrawn carriages to make their way up the narrow gangplank which connected the boat with the shore.

Pam's voice came out a little chokey with excitement. "I can't quite believe it! It's too good to be true."

And Penny exclaimed softly, "It's beautiful! Like something out of another time."

"Don't call her 'it'," Mike corrected, with all the firm assurance engendered by a whole week aboard the *Regina*. "She's a lady. She may not be as young as she once was, but she's still shipshape. That's what Cap Anderson says and he ought to know. He's been sailing for forty years. Quite a guy, the captain. Wait till you meet him."

Mike wasn't taking Harwood's unique summer drama course, as the twins were. He had a job helping the owner of the *Regina* operate the tugboat that propelled the larger craft when she moved from port to port along her scheduled route. His job had made it necessary for him to come directly out from college when the spring term was over and join the captain on the showboat. There had been a lot of preliminary work to do before the summer crop of students arrived. By this time, Pam supposed, practically everyone must be here. But she and Penny had a good reason for being late. And it didn't really matter since her own part in the first production was small and Penny didn't have one. Besides there were still five days till opening night.

As Penny and Pam leaned eagerly forward, savoring their first exciting glimpse of the *Regina*, their animated young faces were so alike in feature and expression that it would have been hard for a stranger to tell them apart. Mike, however, knew well which one was Penny. His hand reached out to close around hers warmly. But although he was a good-looking young man, tall and with hair so blond it shone silver-gilt in the June sunshine, and although Penny was in love with him, she wasn't looking at him now. Her fingers gave his a responsive squeeze, but her fascinated gaze, like that of her twin, remained fixed on the showboat.

"It's so wonderful," Pam said, "just to think of actually living on a showboat, being in the plays or helping with them, having a part in it all."

Penny nodded agreement, her gray eyes alight. But it wasn't, Pam knew, that Penny was as mad about dra-

8

matics as she. Penny was just delighted to have a chance to spend the summer near Mike, seeing him every day, sharing her free time with him. Of course the picturesqueness of the showboat drama course appealed to her, but it was really a secondary consideration, while to Pam it was completely enthralling.

Mike said drily, "It's swell all right, but just don't go expecting too many conveniences. The living quarters are pretty cramped, to put it mildly. And the water system's from the dark ages. It's so scarce we practically have to ration it."

"With all that water around?" Penny gestured.

But Pam wrinkled her nose. "The river looks dirty, though."

"It is," Mike dismissed that particular portion of the Ohio flatly. "Of course, we connect our tank with the town's water supply whenever we tie up. So we get plenty to drink. But when it comes to baths—brother! We almost have to take 'em in a teacup. Except," he amended, in response to Pam's and Penny's worried looks, "that they've rented a room at the girls' club here so that all you females have access to a shower, at least. And the guys can patronize the local Y. So it isn't too bad."

"And after all," Penny reminded, "we were warned when we signed up for the course that showboats didn't come equipped with all the latest improvements."

"Details!" Pam said, with a casual little shrug.

"That's the spirit." Mike grinned at them. "See," he directed their attention to the small squat tugboat connected to the stern of the larger vessel by sturdy braces and a narrow catwalk, "there's the *Dink*. That's what I was hired to help run, although so far I've done more painting and repairing and general handyman jobs than anything else. But when we take off for a new stand, the *Dink*'ll push the *Regina* along."

"That little thing?" Pam exclaimed, as both she and Penny regarded the tug incredulously. "You wouldn't think it could!"

"The *Dink*'s got a diesel motor that's a honey." Mike's

tone was reproving. "Better not let Cap hear you belittle it. Why, the *Dink*'s his pride and joy. Sometimes I think he's even fonder of it than the *Regina*."

It sounded, Pam thought with a slight smile, as though the *Dink* were Mike's pride and joy, too. Why were men always so funny about anything with a motor, she wondered.

She heard Penny voicing the same wistful regret that had tugged at her. "I thought there'd be a regular paddle wheel."

"There is a little one," Mik admitted, chuckling, "but the motor operates it. Anyway, 'm glad it's too much for Cap to handle himself, or I wouldn't be here. I sure couldn't afford to take the showboat course, like you plutocrats."

Penny laughed, her warm glance seeking his face. "We couldn't have afforded it, either, if it weren't for Ty. 'Way back last spring, as soon as he found out how anxious we were to take the course, he insisted on paying our tuition for it."

"He said we should consider it a wedding present from Mother and him," Pam added.

"Didn't he know it's usually the other way around?" Mike teased. "The bride and groom are supposed to get presents from people instead of giving them."

"He knew, all right." Penny nodded. "But that's the way Ty is, nice and generous. He said there was no reason we shouldn't have a summer on a showboat, especilly since Mother and he would be away at least a month of the time on their honeymoon."

"How was the wedding?" Mike remembered to ask then, belatedly. "I hated not to get back to Glenhurst for it, but there was too much work here and a job's a job."

"It was nice," Pam answered, her smiling glance meeting Penny's in a long reminiscent look. "Small, but nice."

"Seems as though we start off every summer with a wedding," Penny added, smiling back at Pam. "Last year Gran's, this year Mother's."

Together their thoughts slipped back over the past few months. It had been in February, during their week at home between college semesters, that Celia Howard had confided to her daughters the not entirely unexpected news that she and Ty Shelton had fallen in love and planned to marry. Ty was a good friend and the head of a furniture company whose line Celia handled through Howard House, her interior decorating shop. Although she had been a widow since the twins were ten, Celia hadn't been quite sure just how they might react to the news. But both Pam and Penny were so fond of Ty, the thought of him as a stepfather had disturbed them not at all. This was particularly true since their mother planned to continue operating Howard House. Nothing, it seemed, was going to be drastically changed by her marriage; there would be no uprooting, no shifting about for the twins. During the period of Celia's and Ty's honeymoon, the shop would be left in the capable hands of her assistant. Upon their return, things should go along much as before, except for Ty's presence. And Ty was such a dear, so droll and warm-hearted, the twins welcomed him into the family as happily as they had welcomed Lucius Clay the previous year when their grandmother had married him.

Pam said, laughing, "With two widows, we needed some men in our family to balance things. Four females were just too much."

"You're not kidding," Mike agreed with the candor of long acquaintance, although there was a teasing gleam in his blue eyes. "A couple of strong male characters should be able to keep you two in line. And if they need any help—"

He broke off at the sound of footsteps crunching the gravel beside the car and they all glanced around to see who was approaching. A tall angular figure in faded Levi's and a striped tee-shirt leaned elbows on the edge of the station wagon window. But it wasn't merely his clothes that gave Professor William Cody Quinn, head of the Harwood College Speech and Drama Department, a most unprofessorial look. His thin, rather homely face lit to rare attractiveness with his smile. His very keen blue eyes peered out from beneath expressive brows, one

11

of which was often cocked higher than the other. And a stubby crew cut made him seem younger than his thirty-five years. Affectionately known as Buff, short for Buffalo Bill, he was the best-liked professor on campus. And his personality, as well as the unusual showboat setup, had combined to make the summer drama course so popular it was hard to get into.

Now Buff Quinn said, grinning in friendly fashion at Pam and Penny, "Welcome to the *Regina*. I see Mike met your train all right."

"Oh, yes," Penny said. "He was the first thing we saw when we got off."

And Pam added, "It's grand to be here."

"Glad to have you," the professor said. He glanced past them at Mike and asked, a little frown pulling his brows closer together, "I take it these were the only showboaters at the station?"

Mike nodded.

Pam asked, surprised, "You mean we're not the last to get here?"

"I wish you were," Buff admitted. "Then my worries would be over. Geneva Day was supposed to arrive yesterday, but there's no sign of her yet, nor any word, either."

"She'll probably get in later today," Mike suggested.

Buff's tone was rather curt. "She'd better. After all, she's got the lead in our opening play."

Mike seemed to have no further words of consolation to offer and neither did Pam nor Penny. They all climbed out of the station wagon and Mike set the twins' two large suitcases and two small ones down onto the ground.

Buff said, sliding in under the wheel, "I've got a couple of errands in town. See you all later."

He drove off with a friendly wave and Mike murmured, shaking his head, "Poor old Buff. He's got more problems! Hope he holds out till opening night."

"He always does," Pam said. She had played parts in several plays at school under Buff's direction. She knew how he invariably worried and fretted in advance and then, when opening night came, the production was as

12

smooth and polished and perfect as his skilled instruction and flair for the drama could make it. "He's always jittery and everything always works out fine."

She turned around to feast her eyes on the showboat once more, dismissing Buff and his troubles from her mind. Penny was gazing at it, too. The soft river breeze blew the twins' dark hair against their cheeks and molded the skirts of their shantung suits about their legs. Penny's suit was navy and Pam's toast brown. They had stopped dressing alike long ago, when the fun of confusing people as to their identity had begun to seem childish. All their friends knew that the more talkative, vivacious twin was Pam, the quieter, but equally poised and assured one was Penny. They were both popular at school, although Pam's friends were a more frivolous and sophisticated crowd than her twin's. But the difference in their personalities didn't in the least interfere with their closeness.

"Come on," Mike said, picking up the two big bags as Pam and Penny took their smaller train cases. "Let's go aboard where you can really see this showboat."

Following him down the steep embankment and then across the narrow wooden gangplank to the *Regina*, Pam felt her heart beat faster and excitement throb in her throat. Being here was like a dream—a wonderful, incredible dream! And it was just starting.

CHAPTER TWO

WELCOME TO THE "REGINA"

EVEN THE COLLEGE CATALOGUE listing of the course had been intriguing. "Operating Theater Aboard the *Showboat Regina*." What a vista the mere words had opened up! Showboats were not among the things one expected to encounter in real life. They were of the stuff of history, fascinating to read about, or to see reconstructed on the stage. However, the twins had discovered, at Harwood College one particular showboat was very real indeed.

They had listened in fascination to all they heard of it, had read every detail supplied in the college bulletin. Captain Oscar Anderson had owned and operated the *Regina* for years. But as he grew old, the responsibility of the whole enterprise had become too much for him. Several years before the twins' enrollment at Harwood, Buff Quinn, casting about for something new in the way of a summer drama course, had hit upon the idea of leasing the showboat. Captain Anderson had charge only of running it, the rest was up to Buff and the students who took the course. These latter paid tuition and received full academic credit for their summer's studies. But their classroom was the showboat and the broad reaches of the Ohio River. There were no formal class periods, no textbooks to pore over. Instead, the course afforded a unique experience for the students involved, helping them learn to live and work together in the best tradition of the old traveling theater. Most of their waking hours were devoted to putting on a good show, one that would attract paying audiences at all the towns they visited. They played parts in the old-fashioned melodramas that were the showboat's natural form of entertainment and did turns in the vaudeville shows that followed. But in addition, each student was a highly responsible citizen of the tight little showboat community, taking over a share of the unpleasant tasks as well as the more glamorous ones. Deck swabbing and kitchen police, costume design and care, scene shifting, advertising, bookkeeping and cleaning the auditorium, all these jobs and many others went into the enterprise. And Professor Quinn saw to it that this fact was clearly understood by prospective students.

Countless gab-sessions in the dorm where Penny and Pam lived had centered around the showboat. Girls who had taken the course were more than willing to spin stories about things that had happened. Difficulties and disasters. Triumphs and spectacular boo-boos. Romances that had blossomed and died or developed into engage-

14

ments. Feuds that had threatened to disrupt the very fabric of showboat life.

Everybody agreed that Buff was wonderful, that they didn't see how he handled it all so successfully. He had an assistant professor, a housemother and a dietician on his staff, still the main responsibility was his. He had to choose wisely among the students clamoring to take the course, not only with an eye to their dramatic ability, but also for their knack of adjusting to other people, of getting along agreeably. And yet, in spite of all his care, clashes had developed on occasion, unforeseen problems of temper and temperament had arisen. But all this only served to make the showboat cruise seem more exciting.

Pam had wanted desperately from the first to enroll for the course. Penny's interest had mounted when Mike got his summer job helping Captain Anderson. But neither girl had much hope of actually getting to go. There was the matter of money—not too plentiful with both of them in college at once. There was also the fact that they wouldn't leave their mother alone all summer, when she could use their help at Howard House. But fate, in the form of a brand-new and generous stepfather, had ironed out every apparently insurmountable obstacle. And now the worn planks of the showboat's deck were at last real and solid under their feet.

Pam sighed a small ecstatic sigh. "Show us everything!" she exclaimed as Mike set down their bags with a thump.

"Everything!" Penny echoed.

"Sure," Mike said. "But these suitcases weigh a ton. What you got in them, rocks or something?"

"Just clothes," Penny told him. "After all, we'll be here ten weeks."

"Dames!" Mike exclaimed with good-natured con- tempt. "You probably brought along a ton of truck you won't need. Life on a showboat's pretty informal, you're going to find out. Levi's and shorts and stuff's all you'll wear."

"That's practically all we brought," Pam informed him.

Just then red-headed Tip Flanders, a particular friend of Pam's, drawn by the sound of their voices, came tearing

15

out of the little office back of the ticket window. Tip had been voted one of the ten best-dressed girls on campus, but you'd never suspect it at the moment. Her once-white sleeveless shirt was soiled and crumpled and her jeans were rolled just below her knees. Moreover, she had apparently sunburned her face quite recently and it was shiny with protective cream.

"Pam, honey!" she exclaimed, beaming and giving Pam a warm welcoming hug. "I thought you'd never get here! Hi, Penny. Gee, it's swell to see you two!"

As the three girls and Mike stood talking, more and more people joined them until almost the whole showboat crew was congregated round about. Ellen Carr, small and dark-haired and quiet, who was Penny's special friend, stood arm in arm with her. There was much laughter and kidding. A wonderful spirit of camaraderie seemed to prevail among all the students and the staff as well. Mrs. Marley, the plump and agreeable white-haired housemother, and Miss Lucy Tidings, the dietitian, who taught Home Ec at Harwood and whom everyone aboard the *Regina* affectionately called Aunt Lucy, joined in to welcome the twins aboard. Aunt Lucy had a dry, but not unkind wit that seemed quite in keeping with her thin form and the braids of dark hair that crowned her rather sharp-featured face.

It was she who remarked finally, "You both look far too civilized for your surroundings. Before you inspect the boat, I suggest someone takes you up to the Hen Roost where you can get into more casual clothes. We're not used to stockings and high heels on the *Regina*."

"That's a good idea," Pam and Penny agreed almost in one breath. Both of them had noted the other girls' shorts and sloppy moccasins, the halters that left their tanned backs bare. Some were barefooted and several had their hair tied back into cool pony tails.

Pam added, smiling, her rueful glance going to her own and Penny's smart suits, "Then we'll feel more at home among the rest of you natives."

"Right this way." Tip Flanders drew Pam along toward the stairway that led to the upper deck. Ellen

16

Carr followed with Penny. And Mike and another boy brought up the rear, carrying the luggage. Talking and laughing they climbed the narrow wooden stairs and moved down the short passageway toward the girls' dorm.

"Prepare yourselves for a shock, kids," Mike warned. "The Hen Roost's like nothing else on earth. I only peeked in once, but the memory will stay with me till my dying day."

"Shame on you!" Tip admonished in mock horror. "You're not supposed to peek in. The Roost's off limits for anyone but us females."

"Yeah," Mike said, "except when there are bags to be carried up and stuff like that. That's when I've seen it. And it's an even bigger mess than the Man Hole."

Tip admitted, "Naturally twelve girls living together make more clutter than an equal number of men. Look how much more paraphernalia girls have."

"You're not kidding," Mike agreed. "Only junk's a shorter word for it."

They had reached their destination. Tip opened the door and took a hasty look inside. "Set the luggage down out here," she suggested to Mike and the other boy. "Then you won't have your delicate male sensibilities upset."

The two boys did as directed. "There you are, kids," Mike said. As he turned to go back downstairs he gave Penny a little hug and suggested, "Let me know when you're ready and I'll take you and Pam on a regular tour of inspection."

"We will." Penny smiled up at him. "And thanks." She followed Pam and the other girls through the doorway.

The Hen Roost was a large, untidy cabin occupying the whole front part of the upper deck. Three of its walls were lined with bunk beds and these were made up neatly. But clothes hung everywhere, the several dressers were crowded with cosmetics and combs and hairbrushes. There were snapshots stuck around the edges of mirrors and stuffed animals lay on the pillows or were flung casually on the floor. Shoes protruded from beneath

17

every bed. All the litter and upheaval of a crowd of girls living in close and uninhibited proximity were plain to see. But none of it bothered Pam or Penny. It just looked cozy and lived-in and inviting. There was an open door at the front of the big room, leading out onto a railed sunny deck, which was furnished with several canvas deck chairs and a battered chaise longue.

"Our veranda," Tip Flanders, who had been keeping up a running comment, informed the twins, with an airy gesture toward the open deck. "Only don't make the mistake of thinking for a minute that it's private."

She and Ellen laughed together and Ellen added, "I wandered out there in my p-js yesterday morning and there were a bunch of kids staring at me from the shore. I had to brush my teeth at them to make them go away."

Tip and Ellen lingered companionably while the twins did a little unpacking and changed their clothes. Conversation bubbled among them, questions and answers overlapped each other. Ellen and Tip were eager to hear all the details of Celia Howard's wedding, of her and Ty's departure on their honeymoon cruise. And the twins were happily willing to supply them.

"It's all so romantic!" Tip exclaimed. "I mean—well, most people's parents have been married forever, so their relationship seems more comfortable than exciting. But to have your mother a bride—and a new stepfather who's as swell as yours sounds, and to get to go to their wedding—" she smiled, "It sounds like fun!"

"It was," Pam admitted, buttoning the belt of her yellow denim shorts.

"Also," Penny added, looking up from the play shoe she was tying, "it's going to be fun to have the regulation number of parents."

"That boy you used to like," Tip remembered suddenly, her inquiring glance on Pam. "What was his name —Randy? Did you get to see him when you were home?"

"He was at the wedding," Pam told her. "His parents and Mother are good friends."

"How was it, seeing him again?" Tip pressed.

18

"Randy and I were all finished long ago," Pam said. "It was just high-school stuff. I told you that before."

"I know." Her friend nodded. "But I thought maybe being together again had fanned the ashes."

"Not a spark," Pam assured her, laughing. "He and I are just old friends now."

She thought, And it would take more than an old friend to make me forget Jeff.

Just the memory of Jeff Moore made a warm little glow burn in Pam. When she had first met Jeff at college, his quiet sincerity and dependability hadn't made much impression on her. There had been other men more dazzling on short acquaintance, but Jeff was the one to whom she turned finally, whose attraction proved strongest and most lasting.

Tip said, with a little wondering shake of her bright head, "I can tell by that gleam in your eye you're thinking of Jeff Moore. There must be something to that old saying about opposites attracting each other. I just can't imagine a smooth character like you really going all out for that big farmer."

Pam smiled faintly, thinking, You just don't know him well enough to appreciate him.

Nor was Tip ever likely to. She wasn't the type Jeff cared for, any more than he was the sort who appealed to her. And yet, Pam realized, in some ways she herself resembled Tip a little. They both liked gay times and amusing people and being popular with their quite sophisticated crowd. But Jeff thought she'd outgrow this attitude in time, whereas he considered Tip a mental lightweight who'd never be very sensible.

Aloud, Pam answered Tip's comment merely, "Nothing wrong with farmers, if they're all like Jeff."

"That's how I feel, too," Penny seconded, her glance warm with approval on her twin's face. Jeff was a good friend of Mike's and Penny's. They had been delighted when he and Pam became interested in each other. Now Penny's voice hurried on eagerly, "But tell us more about the *Regina*."

"She's a nice old tub," Tip drawled, "when you get

19

used to her. She has a certain charm, although it's hard to detect when we're falling all over each other around here."

"You know we're all crazy about her," Ellen's quiet voice was reproachful, "even after only a couple of days on board. She may be old and inconvenient and crowded, but when we actually open and start giving plays, it'll be wonderful."

"I suppose it will be better after opening night," Tip conceded. "Buff's rehearsing us all to death right now. And naturally he's pretty edgy over Geneva's being late."

Ellen wrinkled her small nose expressively. "If it weren't that she's cast as Clarabelle in our first play, she could get lost en route and I'd never miss her."

"How you talk," Pam admonished lightly. "Aren't we all supposed to be just one big happy family around here?"

"Even so," Tip backed Ellen up, "there are some I'd rather be kinfolks with than others. And you know Gen Davis."

"Not very well," Pam admitted. "After all, she's a senior and our paths haven't happened to cross."

"Lucky you," Ellen said and Pam felt a stab of surprise because mild little Ellen certainly wasn't the catty type. She added bluntly, "But you won't be able to keep it that way, not on the showboat . . ."

CHAPTER THREE

MEETING

Buff GAVE THE TWINS the remainder of their first day aboard to get settled and learn their way around the *Regina*, to do their unpacking and take care of any other preliminaries. With Mike acting as guide, they started out to explore the boat from stem to stern, exclaiming enthusiastically over all they saw. They found the old-fashioned auditorium fascinating. With its balcony and box seats, its surprisingly large main floor, it took up the greater part of the *Regina*'s whole area.

"It seats more than four hundred," Mike informed them, "and Buff says we usually have to turn some of the crowd away. People in these old river towns wait for the showboat just as their parents and grandparents used to. Even with movies and all the other modern competition, there's something about a live show that draws them. And besides, the *Regina* herself is quite an attraction."

"I can see that." Penny smiled up at him. Her hand was clasped in Mike's and a warm aura of happiness at being together again seemed to hover about them visibly.

Seeing them thus, Pam felt a sharp stab of loneliness for Jeff, a recurring regret that he, too, couldn't have spent this summer on the showboat. Then it would have been quite perfect. But Jeff hadn't even considered it. He was a few years older than Pam, a veteran who had come to college after serving with the Marines. His summer would be spent working on his parents' farm, which was located close enough to Harwood so that Jeff commuted back and forth to college when classes were in session.

Thinking of Jeff driving around in his disreputable old pickup truck, a soft little smile curved Pam's mouth. She remembered his teasing, "You won't miss me at all on the showboat. You're such a little ham, all it takes to make you happy is a playscript in your hand."

Even as she had denied this, she had realized there was a grain of truth in Jeff's words. She had developed quite a flair for drama under Buff Quinn's skilled instruction in speech class. It had been by far her favorite subject and she had done well in it. Buff had commended her often and she had been rewarded, too, by winning parts in several drama department plays, although freshmen didn't usually do too well in highly competitive tryouts.

Pam had argued with Jeff that he was mistaken, that she would miss him dreadfully. "Just because I love acting doesn't mean I'm going to forget you."

"Better not," Jeff had said, his voice a little gruff the way it sometimes got when he was serious.

And Pam could remember so clearly how he had pulled her close and kissed her, and the special meaning his kiss had seemed to have. The memory of his words came to her, too, almost as though he stood beside her now, tall and solidly built, his brown hair close-cropped, his hazel eyes looking down deeply into hers. "I couldn't forget you, whether we're together or not. But I'm no actor and I've got a farm to help run. Dad's not so young any more. Besides—" Jeff had paused for a moment, as though considering how best to word what he had to say next, "much as I'll hate it, I think it's probably a good thing for us to be apart for a while. We've seen a lot of each other these last few months. This'll give us a chance to get our bearings, to learn how much it all really means."

Pam had agreed with him then, sensibly. But now how that didn't help to dull the edge of her loneliness right now.

She became abruptly aware of Mike's voice, saying, "You know Alan Richmond, don't you, Pam?"

She snapped back to the present with a start. They were standing on the stage of the auditorium, although Pam had no conscious memory of having made her way there with Penny and Mike. And one of the most attractive young men she had ever encountered was standing facing them, a paintbrush in one hand and a friendly grin on his dark and debonair face.

"Hi," Alan Richmond greeted her. "I don't think we've ever actually met, although I've seen you around campus."

Pam acknowledged Mike's introduction with an answering smile. Alan Richmond had black hair with just a hint of wave in it. His interested dark gaze rested appreciatively on Pam. She had noticed him around school, too, as what girl wouldn't? Even in paint-streaked Levi's and an old plaid shirt, the sleeves rolled up on his tanned muscular arms, there was something theatrical and exciting about him. Like someone in the movies, Pam thought. No one specific, just a sort of composite type made up of all the swashbuckling hero-villains of historical dramas.

22

She smiled faintly at the absurdity of her train of thought. Alan was a senior and since seniors weren't prone to waste their attention on freshmen girls, Pam had had no contact with him whatever. Besides, hadn't he spent a good deal of his time in the company of Geneva Day? The memory of the two of them together flashed through Pam's mind.

Something in the way Alan was looking at her made Pam wonder if things mightn't be different on the showboat than they had been at school. She would have been less than human if her heart hadn't hurried a little faster as they lingered there, talking.

Mike said, "I'm taking the girls on a full-scale tour of inspection. They haven't really seen the boat yet."

Alan thrust his paintbrush back into the can and waved distastefully toward the piece of scenery he had been working on. "This is a part of showboat life I could very easily do without," he announced. "And there's absolutely no rush on it. So how about my joining you and helping show the girls around?"

"Sure," Mike agreed, "if you like."

As they went through the two small backstage dressing rooms, in which the entire cast must make costume changes, Alan told Pam, chuckling, "Think what these will be like when a play's going on. Brother, what a ball!"

"It'll be cozy," Pam admitted, laughing.

Mike and Alan conducted the twins through the dining cabin and the galley, the ticket-and-business office, where the showboat's records of profit or loss were kept. They inspected the *Dink*, with its sleek diesel motor and little fore-cabin where some of the boys who were ham-radio enthusiasts had set up a station and from which they got in contact with other hams. On the *Dink*, also, were Captain Anderson's living quarters, the door to which was lettered imposingly, CAPTAIN, PRIVATE. Together the four of them climbed to the second deck of the *Regina* and then one flight above that to where the flat top of the showboat afforded a big sun deck with the pilothouse thrusting up above it in solitary aloofness.

"Cap's up there now," Mike said. "I want you to meet him."

The pilothouse was small and compact and spotlessly clean, its brasswork polished to a fine glow, its wood gleaming with the soft patina of years. Captain Anderson sat in his comfortably cushioned swivel chair, his feet high on a window ledge, his old white cap set jauntily on his equally white head. He had a weathered red face and the brightest blue eyes Pam had ever seen. And when he spoke, after taking an unlit corncob pipe from his mouth, his voice was slow and drawling with an accent curiously compounded of Swedish singsong and Deep South.

It was at once apparent that genuine liking and understanding existed between him and Mike. And the captain's manner indicated plainly that an friend of his young assistant's was a friend of his well. As such he made them welcome in this little private world, with its great pilot wheel and the shining clear windows from which one could look out in all directions across the great wide river.

Somehow a sense of peace and calm welled up in Pam in these surroundings. And she knew Penny was experiencing the same sensation when she said, her voice soft with wonder, "It's like being in a different time up here, a different century."

Cap nodded his white-maned head in agreement and said with a little chuckle, "I can shut the whole twentieth century out of here and spit in its eye, if I want to. And sometimes I feel like doin' it. Wars and rumors of war, atom bombs and destruction, four-lane highways for people to drive like fools on, jet planes dirtyin' up the clear blue sky—when it all gets too much for me, I come up here and wipe the whole troublin' business out of my thoughts as if it was written in chalk and my mind was a blackboard." He added, with a little shake of his head, "Life used to be quieter when I was you kids' age—and calmer and more sensible."

"Not so exciting, though, was it, Cap?" Alan grinned.

"Excitin'!" the old captain positively snorted. "Who needs excitement all the time? That's why people are crackin' up with nerves and havin' to spend money to

24

lie around on psychiatrists' couches, spoutin' about phobias and frustrations! If they'd just simmer down and take time to enjoy the great big beautiful world God made for 'em, they wouldn't be in such a state!"

"I'll still take the present," Alan argued good-humoredly. "The gay nineties may have been all right in their way but I like things to move at a faster pace."

"Why?" Captain Anderson demanded, pointing the stem of his pipe at Alan and pulling his brows together ferociously. "What's so fine about mere speed? People run around in circles nowadays and a lot of 'em never get any farther than they were when they started. But just because they're movin' fast, they figure they're accomplishin' something."

"Now, Cap." Mike grinned at him placatingly. "You know we're not all like that."

"Well, no," the old man admitted. "But too many are. Sometimes I catch myself doin' it and that makes me mad. Then I come up here where it's calm and quiet and get my perspective restored again. It's awful easy," he admitted, "to get so bogged down in trivialities that you ain't got time for important things."

As the lively discussion continued, Pam could see why Mike had wanted them to meet the captain. He was a salty old character, forthright and positive, with a robust wit and a fund of wisdom and common sense that made his arguments hard to answer. Something about him reminded Pam slightly of Lucius Clay, whom Gran had married and of whom they were all so fond. Both men seemed to be turned out of a different, more individual mold than most people nowadays. They were nonconformists, not afraid to think for themselves, even though their opinions might run counterclockwise to the common trend of thought.

Rugged individualists, Pam thought with a little smile. That phrase described them. And their very difference made them interesting. You might not agree with their opinions, still you couldn't help respecting their right to hold them and admiring their candor in voicing them plainly. What a drab, monotone world it would be if

25

everyone thought alike! Such people as Lucius and Captain Anderson were perfect examples of the independent thinking which professors were always advocating and which some of them seemed to fear was in danger of being lost by the present young generation.

The captain had been holding forth at some length on the subject of young people being in too big a rush all the time. Now he demanded, pointing his pipestem at Penny, "Tell me the truth now, young lady! How long's it been since you took time to go for a long leisurely walk in the woods and restore your soul with the sight of a beautiful sunset?"

Before Penny could answer, Mike said good-naturedly, "Quit picking on my girl now, captain. I didn't bring her up here for you to browbeat. She's got real good sense, you'll find out. It's her twin here who's the flibbertigibbet type."

"I like that!" Pam exclaimed laughing.

"Her twin, eh?" The captain's bright blue eyes peered inquiringly from one girl to the other. Then he admitted with a dry little chuckle, "I can't tell 'em apart and that's a fact. But if she's your girl," he glanced at Penny, "then she must have pretty good sense."

"Naturally," Mike agreed, his arm across Penny's shoulders.

When they left the pilothouse a little later, Penny exclaimed enthusiastically, "I like the captain. He's wonderful!"

And Pam nodded. "He reminds me a little of Lucius."

"Yes, he does," Penny agreed. "Something about his manner, rather than his looks."

Mike said, "Wait till he gets started sometime telling you about the real old showboat days. It's fascinating."

Alan said with a faint grin, "I get a large charge out of the captain. Like to needle him a little once in awhile just to get him going. But he's really a good joe."

"He sure is," Mike said flatly.

Pam wondered if she imagined a slight note of hostility in Mike's tone. Something in his attitude toward

Alan made her suspect that they weren't particularly congenial. Probably nothing so definite as dislike existed between them, still there was evidence of a certain lack of understanding, a failure to see eye to eye on things. Which meant, Pam supposed regretfully, that Penny wouldn't be very keen on Alan, either, since she was so prone to agree with Mike.

Too bad, Pam thought, because I like him myself. I like him quite well. And I rather think he may be going to like me.

There were small signs a girl could read, certain indications of a growing interest on Alan's part. Sensing them, Pam felt excitement and anticipation quicken within her. The thought of Jeff came into her mind, but it didn't dissipate the beginning of the attraction she felt toward Alan. After all, Jeff had wanted them to have this summer apart, he had told her to have fun on the showboat, to enjoy her cruise to the fullest extent. That Alan Richmond was going to have a vital part in her enjoyment, Pam felt quite sure.

As though echoing her thought, Alan said softly, for Pam's ears alone as Penny and Mike moved on ahead of them down the narrow stairway toward the lower deck, "I'm glad you're here, Pam. It's going to be fun. . . ."

CHAPTER FOUR

TWO DAYS TILL OPENING

"WHAT A LIFE for an introvert this would be!" Pam exclaimed, pausing in the act of brushing her hair to stare at two small boys, perched on a tree limb, watching her every move with candid interest.

She stood in the bright sunshine that slanted pleasantly across the upper foredeck of the *Regina*. Behind her the Hen Roost was filled with early morning sounds of girls getting out of their bunks and starting to dress.

"Wouldn't it, though?" Tip Flanders agreed. "Maybe that's why Buff only brings along a bunch of extroverts like us."

Tip sat on the rail near Pam, calmly applying nail polish. She didn't even waste a glance on their interested audience. Both girls wore the rolled-up blue jeans and sleeveless blouses which were almost a uniform for the feminine portion of the showboat crew, particularly during the morning hours.

"Why I bother with this I'll never know," Tip went on, waving her fingers in the air to dry the polish. "I'll probably get stuck with washing dishes or scrubbing the auditorium, or some equally grubby task."

"I helped scrub the auditorium yesterday," Pam informed her. "And a stinking job it was, too. But it's all set now for our opening Saturday night."

Tomorrow would be Saturday, she reali d with a faint jolt of surprise. She and Penny had een on the showboat three days. And in this short tim the routine of the *Regina* had grown natural and familiar. Funny, Pam thought, how quickly you could get used to brushing your teeth over the rail and taking a chill shower from a hose rigged up in a sheltered corner of the afterdeck.   lif was rugged and primitive, but its very difference from the modern way of living made it fascinating and a lot of fun. There was a normal amount of griping over inconveniences, over the work tasks assigned, still the fact that Buff and his staff played no favorites made for a good feeling among the students.

"I'm glad something's set," Tip answered Pam dismally. "The play sure isn't. Did you ever see such a mess, with Geneva still not here?"

"You're telling me?" Pam inquired, lifting a quizzical eyebrow. No one was feeling Geneva's continued absence more than she. Pam had been reading the other girl's part, as well as her own small one, so that the rest of the cast could rehearse around the missing leading lady.

"I don't see why Buff lets her get away with it," Tip growled, putting the cap back on her bottle of nail polish.

"There may be some good reason she's late," Pam said, but she didn't sound too convinced herself. She went on, "Buff says she'll know the part of Clarabelle through and through by this time. He let her take a script with her when she went home to California."

"But to be so late and not even let him know—" Tip began.

A voice interrupted from the door of the Hen Roost behind them. It was Carla Trent, a slim, black-haired girl with a rather sharp tongue that sometimes inflicted hurt. She drawled, "Maybe Buff's leniency is due to the fact that Gen's got a very rich uncle who's been most generous to Harwood in the way of an endowment. Probably Buff feels he can't bite the hand and so on. I'll bet he wouldn't put up with such actions from the rest of us."

"Buff's not like that," Pam argued.

Everyone at Harwood had heard of Geneva Day's uncle, Andrew Mitchell, a school alumnus who had donated a large part of the cost of the new library. But that Buff Quinn would let himself be influenced by that, she couldn't believe.

"Don't be naïve, pet." Carla smiled at her. "It's a hard cruel world and endowments are hard to come by."

"I'd hate to think Buff would butter her up because of that." Tip frowned, adding doubtfully, "But it does seem funny."

Then the breakfast bell rang, loud and clear on the morning air. That, along with the beguiling aroma of bacon and coffee, drew everyone to the sunny dining cabin in record time. There was an animated buzz of conversation, punctuated with laughter and the brisk clatter of dishes and silver, as the meal got under way.

Alan Richmond, who had saved a seat for Pam beside him, said, "Guess what job I drew today."

"You mean you already know?"

Mary Hatcher, an efficient senior who served as the showboat's business manager and had charge of assigning the various jobs, always posted the day's worksheet on

29

the bulletin board right after breakfast. Until then no one usually knew what job was to be his.

Alan nodded, grinning. "I sneaked a peek over Mary's shoulder when she was typing the worksheet. Sort of a preview. I get to drive around and tack up SHOW-BOAT COMING signs along all the roads. And in town I coax stores to put posters in their windows. Cushy job, eh?"

"Not bad," Pam agreed. "With your persuasive charm, it should be simple."

"I even get an assistant," Alan informed her. "Your sister."

"How nice." Pam smiled at him and poured milk over her cereal. She let no hint of the regret she felt, that it hadn't been she instead of Penny, sound in her tone.

She didn't even suppose Penny would appreciate her luck, getting to spend a whole morning driving around with Alan. Penny would rather be with Mike. But every other girl on the *Regina* would be pea-green with envy. There wasn't one of them, and that included Pam herself, who didn't feel the power of Alan's attraction to some degree.

He asked now, leaning confidentially nearer, "I don't suppose you could arrange to swap identities for a while?"

Pam felt a momentary urge of temptation. She and Penny used to do that sometimes. She might be able to persuade her twin. But Pam decided against it almost at once. No reason to let Alan get the idea she was that anxious to be with him.

"That's kid stuff," she told him airily. "Penny and I outgrew pretending we were each other years ago." She asked then, her curiosity prompting her, "You didn't peek enough to know what I'm doing this morning, did you?"

Alan nodded. "Marketing," he answered, "with Rudy Blair."

His tone and his amused dark glance dared her to pretend that she liked her assignment as well as her sis-

30

ter's. So Pam wouldn't give him the satisfaction of seeing her disappointment. Instead she murmured lightly, "Well, that sounds easy enough." Pushing a grocery cart around the super market with plump, good-natured Rudy, might not be exciting, but at least it was preferable to some of the other jobs she might have drawn.

"Yeah," Alan said. Pam thought he sounded just a bit put out as he turned his full attention to his breakfast. But it served him right. No man should be quite so sure of his charm and its effect on the female sex, she reflected with a faint smile.

Later, as Pam stood with Penny and some of the others in front of the bulletin board, she saw that Alan had been right about her morning's job. There was the usual medley of groans and delighted exclamations, depending on which jobs had been assigned. Several girls remarked about Penny's luck.

Tip Flanders moaned, "K. P.! I might have known. Just as sure as I do my nails something foul like that happens to me."

"Rehearsal at eleven," Pam remarked. "That means I'd better find Rudy and get the grocery list from Aunt Lucy in a hurry or we won't be back in time."

People were already beginning to scatter for their various jobs. Morning was a busy time on the *Regina*, and work started early.

Penny confided to Pam, "I wish someone else were going with Alan instead of me. I don't care much about him."

"You're the only girl on board who feels that way," Pam told her. "He's very attractive."

Penny shrugged. "He knows it, though, and that spoils it. He isn't nearly as good-looking as Mike," she added positively.

"Not that you're prejudiced, or anything," Pam teased.

"Well, he isn't," Penny said firmly. "He's not as cute as Jeff, either, nor nearly as nice."

"He may not be as nice," Pam agreed, "but he's certainly more handsome. I'm not so blind I can't see that. He's as good-looking as most movie stars, while Jeff—"

she smiled as the thought of Jeff washed warmly over her heart—"well, he's just Jeff and more than slightly terrific."

Penny gave her elbow a little squeeze. "So long as you feel like that, I guess I needn't worry about you falling for Alan and forgetting Jeff."

Pam shook her head. "You needn't worry."

But as their ways separated, she found herself resenting Penny's attitude just a bit. After all, if she liked Alan, it was her own affair. It had nothing to do with Penny. Just because Mike and Jeff were good friends and Penny, too, liked Jeff a lot, it didn't mean that Pam must spend this whole summer without a man, or a date, or some harmless fun. Having Alan pay attention to her made life more interesting and what was wrong with that? Jeff hadn't tried to impose any restrictions on her, he wanted her to enjoy herself. And Pam intended to do so. Penny needn't hover about like a mother hen with one chick, making her feel guilty if she so much as flirted with Alan.

Penny probably didn't mean to do that, Pam reminded herself in all fairness. It was only natural for her to be interested. They'd always been interested in each other's affairs, not in any objectionable way, just in a warm, natural manner.

I must be getting touchy, Pam thought ruefully.

She decided to go up to the Hen Roost to freshen her lipstick and put on a blouse and skirt, before heading for the galley to pick up the grocery list from Aunt Lucy. Buff felt that the showboat troupe shouldn't dress too casually for their trips into town. It tended to destroy the illusion the townspeople had built up about them as performers.

Performers! Pam thought wryly. Me with my ten-line part! I must be very careful of the impression I make on our future audience.

But it wouldn't be that way always. Buff would surely give her a decent part in some later production. Pam had kept to herself the unhappiness she felt over her meager role in *Virtue Rewarded*. After all, everyone

32

couldn't have the lead. Penny didn't even have a part in the first play. She would merely serve as an usher and sell candy during the intermission. But Penny didn't care. She felt her dramatic ability was negligible. But Pam loved being on stage, she enjoyed every aspect of acting.

She was a ham, just as Jeff had teased. She couldn't truthfully deny it. She felt sure she could have played Clarabelle in the funny old melodrama. She could have done quite as well as Geneva Day. Why, already she knew some of Geneva's lines by heart, just from reading them during the other girl's absence from rehearsals. How could Geneva treat Buff like that, Pam wondered? And she wondered even more why Buff let her get away with it.

Maybe, Pam told herself as she started toward the galley, it was her disappointment at having such a small part, added to her loneliness for Jeff, which had made her ready to flare up over Penny's natural interest. But there was no use taking all her inner frustrations out on poor Penny. Pam was glad she had held her tongue.

She almost ran into Rudy Blair, emerging from the galley with the list in his hand. "Oh," Pam said and smiled, "I see you got it. We'll have to rush or we won't be back in time for rehearsal."

"I know," Rudy said, "so let's get going." His round pink face and dignified, though genial, manner were great assets to him in playing businessmen and bank presidents in the showboat productions. He tucked a friendly hand under Pam's arm and hurried her toward the gangplank.

But just as they reached it, Buff Quinn's voice, calling Pam, stopped them. Curiously she turned around. There was a note of unaccustomed urgency in the young professor's tone and he was frowning.

"Oh, oh!" Rudy murmured into her ear. "Sounds as if you're in bad." He stepped aside to wait for her.

Buff suggested, however, "Better get Mary to detail someone else to help you, Rudy. This may take a while."

Pam couldn't guess why Buff wanted her. She tried to think of anything she'd done, or neglected to do,

33

which might account for her being called onto the carpet. But she was still at a complete loss as she came up to Buff, her eyes lifted inquiringly to his grave face. Buff motioned her ahead of him into the ticket office, deserted at this hour. He closed the door behind them and indicated a chair. Mystified, Pam sat down on the edge of it, while Buff perched on a tall stool opposite her and hitched his moccasin-clad feet through the rungs.

CHAPTER FIVE

A BREAK FOR PAM

"PAM, I'VE GOT A PROBLEM," Buff Quinn began in his rather abrupt way. His lips were set in a grim line and his thoughtful eyes were staring at her, a question buried in their blue depths.

But Pam felt her sense of uneasiness lift. That was no way to start a calling down. It wasn't anything she'd done that accounted for Buff's peremptory summons. More likely it seemed he was about to ask her help.

"It's Geneva Day," Buff said and Pam's interest quickened. "She was due here days ago and the only word I've had was a wire last night saying she'd be a little late. Nothing definite as to the time of her arrival, no explanation. That's Geneva." His mouth twisted in a rather wry grin and he fished a crumpled pack of cigarettes out of his pocket and lit one.

Then all the Hen Roost gossip about Geneva's highhanded, inconsiderate ways had some basis in fact, Pam thought. It wasn't just so much scuttlebutt. Buff sounded as though he might have tangled with Geneva before, as if her present actions weren't too big a surprise to him. But he also sounded angry, as well he might be, and as if his patience had run out.

Pam sat there, gray eyes intent on the professor's troubled face, her heart beginning to beat faster at the mounting suspicion as to what he might possibly be getting at.

Buff went on, leaning forward, elbows on knees, in his earnestness. "You're the quickest study I've got, Pam. And you've been reading Geneva's part, so you're at least slightly familiar with it. There are half a dozen others who could take your part on short notice. But Geneva's is something else." C617019 CO. SCHOOLS

Pam managed to say, around the knot of rising excitement in her throat, "It's the leading part."

"I know." Buff's eyes never left her face. "It's the leading part and a long one. And you've only today and tomorrow to learn it. So if you turn me down cold, I can't blame you. But I'm in a spot, a tough spot, Pam. As you know—and Gen Day knows," he interpolated firmly, "we open tomorrow night. Gen's quite capable of turning up any time, her lines all learned and ready to step into her part. But I can't gamble on it any longer —not and have the whole production thrown for a loop if she doesn't get here. So do you think you can do it, learn the part of Clarabelle and play it with only two days to get ready? I know it's asking a lot."

Pam exclaimed, delight and anticipation making her voice break just a little, "I can—I know I can!" When had anything quite so exciting and wonderful happened to her before?

"Good girl!" Buff sounded as though the weight of the world had just rolled off his shoulders. "I'll have Mary let you off everything else for the time being. Just concentrate on that part. Why don't you go up on the top deck where it's quiet and study till rehearsal? I'll try to get hold of Alan and send him up to cue you. Several of your most important scenes are with him."

Pam knew that. Alan was playing Archibald Sutherland, the villain, in *Virtue Rewarded*. And as the heroine, she would be the main object of his dastardly goings-on. These culminated in his tying her to the railroad track, just before the Midnight Flyer was due, a fate from which the hero managed to rescue her with only seconds to spare.

Pam murmured now, with a faint smile, "He's supposed to put up posters this morning. And I'm supposed to buy groceries. Mary'll hate you, switching everyone's job around."

"No, she won't," Buff said positively. "She knows this is vital. . . ."

And apparently Buff was right. Mary must have given him full co-operation, for Pam had scarcely settled herself in a canvas chair on the sunny, deserted top deck, when Alan Richmond came up the stairs to join her.

Pam looked up from the playscript she had been studying and her eyes met Alan's dark, interested ones.

"Hey!" he exclaimed. "I hear you're the new leading lady."

Pam nodded. "I guess so—if I can learn the part in time." But she didn't sound doubtful and her eyes sparkled with enthusiasm. "I'm glad Buff got hold of you to cue me."

"So am I." Alan grinned and his teeth flashed white in his tanned face. "Mary's schedule is all snafued but she'll work it out. And it's lots more pleasant, spending the morning up here with you than putting up posters with your sister."

"Thanks," Pam said rather absently. Already her eyes were fixed once more on the script. So many speeches to memorize, so much stage business! Old-fashioned melodrama might not call for much finesse, or many delicate shadings of interpretation, but the leading lady certainly had to know her lines. And there was so little time.

Alan's hand covered hers briefly, reassuringly, as though he had read her thought. "Don't worry," he told her, "you can do it. Just tell me one thing before we start. What about Gen? Isn't she coming at all?"

Pam shrugged. "I guess so, but Buff doesn't know when. The wire she sent wasn't very enlightening and he doesn't feel he can take a chance on her not making it by tomorrow night. I suppose"—Pam frowned—"she could turn up any time." The realization gave her a queer, unsettled feeling. "I wonder what Buff would do then?"

"Who knows?" Alan said. "He's fed to the teeth with her and you can't blame him. Lots of the kids have been

36

wondering why he accepted her for the course at all. Gen can be pretty hard to get along with when she puts her mind on it. She can also," Alan added, "be very persuasive."

Pam thought she detected a sudden knowing twist to his grin. The recollection of having seen him with Geneva a good deal around school grew more definite in her mind.

"Anyway," Alan went on, "my guess is that if you know the part by the time Gen condescends to put in her belated appearance, so that Buff's precious production won't suffer, he'll tell her to go fly a kite."

If I know the part, Pam thought.

She had to learn it, and quickly! Not only for her own sake, because playing the leading role was so important to her, but also in order to help Buff put Geneva Day in her place. The other girl had no right to disrupt everything, to leave the whole showboat crew in a spot as she had. It would serve her right and help teach her a well-deserved lesson to arrive and find her part filled, the production going on smoothly without her.

What does she think she is, Pam thought fiercely, indispensable? Aloud, she prodded Alan, "Go on, cue me. . . ."

Never had Pam put in such grueling hours of intensive study as she did the rest of that day. She stumbled through the late morning rehearsal, her script clutched in her perspiring hand, trying hard to refer to it as little as was absolutely necessary. Everyone else in the cast proved helpful and co-operative and Pam was grateful for their attitude and for Buff's patient coaching.

Then there were more hours of concentrated study on her part, and at four o'clock another rehearsal. Pam was much more sure of herself and her lines during this one than she had been in the morning. Her good memory hadn't failed her in an emergency, as she had been half afraid might happen. She still fumbled for a speech here and there and missed an occasional cue, but everyone was more than willing to make allowances and to help her out.

"You're wonderful!" Penny whispered, hugging her as Pam came offstage at the play's end. "I'm so proud of you!"

Pam gave her an appreciative squeeze in return. It was wonderful to have Penny and the others on her side, building up her morale. The final accolade was Buff's laying an encouraging hand on her shoulder after dismissing the cast to get ready for dinner. "You'll make it all right," he told her. "You're doing fine." Pam didn't mind at all when he added, "Later, after you're rested, I'd like to run through that scene at the end of the first act with just you and Alan. There's a couple of kinks there we'll have to straighten out."

"Of course." Pam nodded. She was grateful for Buff's approval. And after she'd eaten she wouldn't feel quite so achingly weary, so ready to collapse in a limp heap.

Even an inadequate sponge bath and a change of clothes helped a little. By the time Pam reached the dining cabin and slid into her place at the long table, she felt almost herself again. Exultation and excitement filled her once more and she took her usual part in the amiable chatter going on around her.

Penny commented, her glance bright with admiration, "I don't see how you do it, learning a whole long part like that in such a short time."

"I haven't learned it yet," Pam admitted, "but I'll get there."

It was nice to bask in Penny's approval, to see the admiring looks on the faces of her friends. Pam had a very human love of spending her share of time in the spotlight. And she felt its beam shining pleasantly on her tonight.

Tip Flanders, who, disguised in a gray wig and grease paint wrinkles, would play the part of Pam's mother, leaned a little closer across the table to tell her, "I hear there's been no further word from the fair Geneva. Buff must be boiling!"

If he was, it didn't show. Pam's glance followed Tip's to the professor who sat at the head of the table, calmly eating his dinner while he engaged in conversation with the housemother, Mrs. Marley. Was he really as relaxed and easy as he appeared, Pam wondered, after having had to put a green substitute into the lead in his opening play?

She asked Tip, "Can you imagine why she'd be so late? It seems if she was interested enough to sign up for the course, and try out for a leading part, she'd make an effort to get here."

"With Gen," Tip said, "it's hard to tell. Something may have turned up unexpectedly that sounded more exciting. The Days are so rich, she may have decided to zoom over to Europe or somewhere for a gay week end while we sit around waiting for her."

"We're not waiting any more," Alan reminded. "The show must go on, to coin a phrase."

"I know," Pam nodded thoughtfully. "But I still can't see why she'd act this way. When she knew Buff was counting on her, that the whole production would be upset if she didn't show up—"

Tip interrupted positively, "That wouldn't matter a lot to Gen. She's the type who always thinks of herself first—and second and third, for that matter."

"Watch it there." Mike leaned over from his seat beyond Penny to warn Tip. "Your claws are showing."

"The subject of our conversation," Tip informed him, "is the type that brings out the cat in any woman."

"Maybe," Penny suggested, "something happened that she couldn't help."

"She could have said so in her wire," Pam pointed out. "She wouldn't have to be so indefinite—" she broke off, aware that a sudden startled hush had fallen on the room. For a second utter silence reigned. Not even the clatter of silver against a dish was audible. Baffled, Pam turned her head to look for the cause.

In the doorway Geneva Day stood, slim and smart in a dark linen suit that set off her long pale hair and dark-lashed aquamarine eyes. A slight smile parted her lovely lips as she said, to everybody in general, while her glance quested about seeking someone in particular, "Well, hello, everybody."

There was a murmur of greeting in answer and underneath it Tip confided to Pam, "An entrance, if I ever saw one!"

Pam's throat felt suddenly tight. She couldn't have spoken if she had had to. All her long hours of study, the grueling rehearsals, the hopes she had allowed to spring up within her that the leading part might really be hers tomorrow night— She drew a deep ragged breath and felt Penny's fingers press hers and knew that her twin was sharing the turbulent sensations welling up in her. It was always like that. Words weren't necessary between them. Being twins gave them a special kind of understanding, even though they were different in so many inner ways. And Pam was glad of Penny's sympathy, her ardent, if unspoken, partisanship now.

Tip whispered, "That little stinker! Just watch her go to work on Buff."

What was it Alan had said that afternoon? Pam's mind groped. Something about how persuasive Geneva could be. Was the dazzling smile she was giving Buff Quinn now a part of her powers of persuasion? She extended her hands eagerly as she moved toward him and her voice was warm and low, exclaiming, "Buff! How wonderful to see you!"

The young professor got to his feet and the look he gave Geneva was long and steady. But Buff's was the sort of face that could hide completely what he was feeling. Nor did his tone give Pam any dependable clue to his reaction as he murmured, "So you finally got here."

"Of course." Geneva smiled appealingly. "You got my wire?" At Buff's nod, she chattered on, "I hated to be so indefinite, but I couldn't say just exactly when I'd be here. You knew I'd make it in time for the opening, though." Her eyes crinkled beguilingly at the corners. "But, you see, there was this big house party in honor of Uncle Andy's birthday. It went on for days and I just couldn't get away any sooner."

Ah, yes, Pam thought. Dear Uncle Andy, the giver of generous endowments. It wouldn't be tactful or politic for Buff to appear indifferent to Uncle Andy's birthday celebration.

Still, he was saying, "You could have made your wire a little more informative."

"I know," Geneva said regretfully. "But by the time I could have let you know definitely when to expect me, I figured I'd get here just about as soon as a wire could. I flew out, of course."

The professor glanced around, aware suddenly of all the fascinated witnesses to his little interchange with Geneva. An enigmatic grin twisted his lips. "Maybe," he said, "we'd better talk this over in the office."

"But I hate interrupting your dinner—" Geneva began.

"Come on." Buff was already moving toward the door. Geneva had to hurry to keep up with his long strides. As they passed from the dining room, Pam heard Geneva assuring Buff, "You needn't worry. I know the part of Clarabelle perfectly."

Pam thought, I don't know it quite that well, so I suppose I'll have to go back to playing Clarabelle's friend who only comes into a couple of short scenes.

The taste of disappointment was bitter in her mouth. Even the hearty assurances of Mike and Penny and Tip that Buff wouldn't let Geneva get around him didn't help. Pam was aware of the inner uncertainty that made them all protest too much.

Alan Richmond leaned over to say confidentially, "It's a dirty deal, after all the work you've put in today."

"You, too," Pam murmured, trying to smile, "feeding me all those cues. I guess—we both wasted a lot of time."

Buff's primary concern would be for the success of his opening production. That was only natural, Pam reasoned with herself. Look at all the time and effort that had gone into it, all the tickets that had been sold, all the people who would be disappointed if the show wasn't good. It was easy to view the situation sensibly and realistically. Just the same, Pam found that her appetite for the rest of her dinner had disappeared entirely.

41

CHAPTER SIX

BUFF MAKES A DECISION

PAM COULD MAKE ONLY a feeble pretense of eating. Pushing her food around on her plate might fool the others, but she was well aware that Penny saw through her. If only Tip and the rest would stop trying so obviously to be reassuring! They meant it in a kindly, helpful way, Pam knew, but kicking the subject around only made her feel worse. And the longer Geneva and Buff stayed away, the heavier grew Pam's sense of defeat and disappointment.

After dinner she managed to elude everyone. Penny was sharply conscious of her desire to be alone, so she made no effort to intrude on her twin's privacy. Pam slipped like a wraith through the blue dusk to a deserted angle of the upper deck and leaned there, elbows on the broad wooden rail.

Far across the river, lights were springing on among the darkening trees that climbed upward from the river bank. Houses were over there, Pam knew, and stores and street lights—another city in a different state, since the river formed the dividing line. A city filled with people whom Pam had never seen, each individual with his personal problems, happiness, trouble. But they were unreal to Pam, remote across the broad Ohio. She felt entirely detached from them, filled with her own sharp misery.

Farther down the river, she glimpsed the great steel and stone span of the bridge. It looked thin and cobwebby at this distance, etched against the dusky sky. The lights flashing constantly across it were car headlights, Pam knew, yet they might have been toys, so tiny they seemed. She lifted her eyes from the man-made brilliance of the lights to the gray dome of the evening sky, where a single star hung. A part of her was aware of its chaste imperturbable beauty, but nothing could really distract her attention from her own problem.

It was useless to try to pretend it didn't matter if Geneva got back the leading part. It did matter. It mattered dreadfully to Pam. She tried to find some cheer in the knowledge that she wouldn't, actually, be any worse off than she would have been if Geneva had simply arrived when she was supposed to and Pam had been left in her small supporting part. But that wasn't really true. She had had this day of hope, of working hard toward perfecting her lines. She had dreamed a shining dream of herself in the role of Clarabelle tomorrow night, the spotlight bright in her eyes, the heady sound of applause in her ears. And by that time she could have played the lead as well as Geneva. Pam was sure of it.

If only, she thought, Geneva hadn't come till tomorrow! If only her plane had been grounded somewhere, so she'd have been too late!

But the plane hadn't been grounded. And Geneva was down in the office right now, using all her wiles on Buff, wrapping him around her finger. And there was nothing Pam could do, except lean here on the *Regina*'s worn rail and eat her heart out. The decision was Buff's to make and Pam had very little hope he'd decide in her favor.

How long she remained there in the deepening dark, Pam had no idea. Soft noises murmured about her, the creak of old wood, the gentle sucking of water at the showboat's sides, an occasional muted voice or laugh in the distance, but she didn't hear them. At last there was a sound of footsteps approaching along the deck behind her and she turned, trying to blink away the tears that she had so far managed to hold back. As she had half expected, it was Penny.

"Pam," her sister's voice was low, "Buff's looking for you."

Pam nodded and followed Penny wordlessly back to the narrow stairway. As they descended, Pam asked,

"You—don't know what he's decided?" Maybe it would be easier if Penny could break the bad news to her.

But Penny admitted sympathetically, "No, he didn't say."

It's only a part in a play, Pam tried to reason with herself sensibly. It won't mean the end of the world if I don't get it. I should have known better than to set my heart on it so.

As they reached the bottom of the stairway, the twins were met by a slim, well-groomed figure in a dark suit and high heels that clicked with staccato emphasis on the wooden deck. Pam's eyes lifted in surprise to stare directly into Geneva Day's face as she stood aside impatiently to let them pass before she mounted the stairs, apparently on her way to the Hen Roost.

Geneva's lovely mouth was set in a thin straight line and for an unguarded moment sheer hate looked out of her clear aquamarine eyes. Pam felt the impact of her look as though it were a physical blow and sensed its significance even before Geneva spoke. "Buff tells me you've taken over my part. Congratulations."

Pam could do no more than murmur, "Why, thanks —but I'm sorry you—" when the other girl swept disdainfully past and mounted the stairs swiftly with her light graceful step. If she had told Pam to shut up, her meaning couldn't have been any clearer. Pam felt hot color flame across her face.

Penny's fingers tightened on hers. Penny's voice was low and delighted in her ears. "He didn't give it to her!" she whispered. "Oh, Pam, I'm so glad for you! Everyone will be!"

Pam was glad, too. Already happy relief was beginning to spread through her. But she was still shaken by the venomous look Geneva had given her, the insult implicit in the way she had brushed past both of them, as though they were of no account. Had Penny seen it, sensed it, too, Pam wondered?

As her questioning glance met that of her twin, Pam had her answer. Both of them knew that Buff, by hold-

ing out against Geneva and doing the fair thing, had
made an implacable enemy for Pam.

CHAPTER SEVEN

OPENING NIGHT

SATURDAY WAS PROBABLY the busiest day, certainly the
most exciting, that Pam had ever spent. There were
rehearsals and costume fittings, endless study of her lines
until she felt sure she could have said them backward as
well as forward.

"You'll be all right," Buff assured her half a dozen
times. "Don't worry."

In the back of Pam's mind the memory of her talk
with Buff last night glowed like a bright flame. It hadn't
been a long talk. Buff had told her simply that she was
to keep the leading part, that he had made very plain to
Geneva the reasons for the switch.

"If a person's not dependable in a setup such as we
have here on the showboat," he had told Pam, "she's of
no earthly use. I'm giving Gen another chance to prove
she's got what it takes. But I certainly wouldn't let you
down after all the work you've put in." He had grinned
at Pam then, demanding, "You didn't think I would,
did you?"

"I was worried," Pam had admitted frankly. "I knew
you'd have to do what was best for the production."

"You can swing the part fine." For a moment Buff's
hand had rested hearteningly on her shoulder. "The production will go off just as well as it would with Gen
in it."

How could you let a guy like that down?

Buff had said nothing more about Geneva, about the
stormy scene that had probably taken place between
them. And Pam had thought it wise not to ask questions. Better, she had felt, to let the matter drop and
hope that Geneva's resentment would be short-lived.

Pam was glad, Saturday morning, to learn that while Geneva wouldn't appear in the opening play at all, she would do a song-and-dance routine in the vaudeville show that followed. Gen had taken dancing lessons for years, she was quite professional in the ease and grace with which she danced before an audience. So her pride shouldn't suffer too greatly, Pam hoped.

Still, all that busy, hectic Saturday, Pam was sharply aware of the other girl's anger whenever they encountered each other. Geneva tried to disguise it, yet it flared in her eyes and sharpened the tone of her voice.

Pam confided to Penny, "She absolutely hates me."

"I guess she's still pretty mad," Penny sounded troubled. "But she'll get over it."

"I'm glad she isn't in the play," Pam said. "The way she feels right now, I wouldn't put it past her to try to throw me off my lines by giving me a wrong cue."

"Buff would really bounce her then," Penny said. "I understand she's sort of on probation, so I expect she'll behave herself. She must want to stay on the showboat, or she wouldn't have bothered coming at all."

"I suppose so." Pam nodded.

But she had a strong hunch that Gen Day was not an easy person to fathom. Even knowing her so slightly, Pam sensed currents and crosscurrents in the other girl's nature, urges and impulses pulling her different ways. Alan, who knew her better, had implied that such was the case.

"I expect," Pam told Penny with a faint smile, "I'd better just stay out of her way as much as possible till she's had time to cool off!"

Excitement mounted gradually all that day aboard the *Regina*. Opening night—what a magic flavor the very words had! There was a glitter and glamour about them that sang in the blood and made the heart beat faster. Would the play be a hit? Everyone was wondering. Would all the seats be sold out? Thanks to their advance advertising and the radio interviews with various members of the cast on the local station, more than half of the available tickets had been sold. But what of the other two hundred or so?

"Wait till after the parade," Buff told them all confidently. "That'll take care of the rest of the tickets. We'll probably be turning people away before curtain time."

He gave Pam some time off from her studying to take part in the parade. "The break will do you good," he said, "blow the cobwebs out of your brain. Besides, no one should miss the first parade of the season."

In the crowded, noisy Hen Roost, Pam donned one of the Clarabelle costumes, a wide-skirted black-and-white checked gingham, over voluminous crinoline petticoats. She tied the red satin bow of an old-fashioned flower-trimmed poke bonnet coquettishly under her chin. Penny wore pink, over demurely lace-ruffled pantaloons. All about, the rest of the girls were getting into similar costumes.

When the parade started out, a six-piece band wearing bright red trousers and white shirts, blew lustily on cornets and trumpets and beat the big bass drum. Geneva Day, in short white skirt and towering red shako led them, as drum majorette, strutting and twirling her glittering baton. All the rest of the showboaters followed in costume, the boys decked out in tight trousers and tail coats, or in ludicrous baggy pants and wide flaring bow ties, that they wore for the vaudeville performance. Alan Richmond was garbed as the traditional old-time villain, complete with high silk hat and a dramatic, scarlet-lined black cape. He twisted his black moustache and leered about fiendishly as he slunk along. Bringing up the rear of the procession was Buff Quinn and his assistant Bob Sinclair, riding in the crepe paper bedecked station wagon and ballyhooing the showboat through a portable loudspeaker.

Pam knew she'd never forget how people stood, laughing and calling out to them, cheering them on as they marched down the town's main street. Some of the magic of real showboat days seemed to have spilled over into the present, drawing it and the past close together.

47

And afterwards there was quite a run on the box office, just as Buff had predicted, proving that this old-fashioned method of direct advertising was still effective.

Dinner was hazy in Pam's mind. She supposed she ate, but she had no idea what the meal consisted of. Probably everyone else was in the same state. Tension built up higher and higher as the hour of the performance drew near. "Take it easy," people kept telling each other, but no one paid much attention. The cast and ushers, the vendors of soft drinks and candy and popcorn, were all in costume. Buff leaned on the foredeck railing, apparently quite cool and calm.

"Inside, though," Mary Hatcher confided to Pam, "he's about to pop. He's always like that the night we open."

Pam could spare only the topmost layer of her attention to Buff. She gulped, "Mary, what if I get confused in that scene where Alan ties me to the railroad track and forget—"

"You won't," Mary interrupted positively. "Don't worry."

Penny came hurrying up, her eyes bright with excitement. She wore the brief, stiffened black skirt and trim red weskit of an usher and her make-up was quite superfluous, so pink were her cheeks with anticipation.

"Pam," she exclaimed, catching her sister's hand, "come on up top where you can see! The calliope concert's about to start."

Before living on the showboat and talking with Cap Anderson, Pam hadn't known that playing a calliope took a strong pair of hands and wrists and quite a lot of practice. The organ-like instrument was equipped with whistles operated by steam and had a small keyboard. As the steam pressure mounted, with more and more coal being shoveled to raise it, the keys became harder to push down and the music resulting grew higher and shriller. According to the captain a calliope could be heard six miles away.

Now, as Pam and Penny and half a dozen others stood watching and listening, and as a crowd began to gather on shore in the early dusk, Rudy Blair, earnest and per-

spiring, played one lively old tune after another to enthusiastic applause.

"Look at poor Mike," Penny said, pointing downward
toward the deck of the *Dink*.

Pam's glance followed her sister's finger. Stripped to
the waist and streaked with sweat and coal dust, Mike
was shoveling fuel into the steam engine's hopper, so that
Rudy, high above him on the *Regina*'s upper deck, could
produce what calliope enthusiasts would call music.

"I'll bet he's glad there's only half an hour's concert
before each performance." Pam smiled.

It was still light when Rudy had finished, but a large
crowd had assembled and now people began climbing
the gangplank to the showboat's deck and were ushered
to their seats in the auditorium. Penny was busy with
her duties, but Pam, keyed-up and tense as curtain time
drew inexorably nearer, lingered alone on the upper deck.
She hoped to gain some measure of composure from the
pale dusk and the gentle lap of river water against the old
boat's sides. How could she go on, with her throat feeling
cotton dry and her mind quite blank and empty?

Presently she was joined by Alan, looking strange in
his false moustache and dashing villain's costume. But
then, Pam realized, she must not look entirely natural
herself, in Clarabelle's billowing skirts and flower-trimmed
straw bonnet.

The thought made her smile, as she murmured, "Aren't
we a pair, though?"

Alan grinned back at her. "Those clothes are becoming to you. They had the right idea in the gay nineties.
Women really looked like women in all those ruffles and
stuff."

"And you could always tell a villain by his red-lined
cape," Pam carried the idea on lightly.

They talked nonsense for a few minutes and Pam's
jitters began to abate, she felt easier and more relaxed.
Then a suspicion struck her. "Did you come up here
just to help me get un-kinked?" she demanded.

Alan laughed, admitting, "Something like that. I was

49

afraid you'd fly apart before curtain time if you didn't calm down."

"Buff sent you, I'll bet!" Pam accused.

But Alan denied this firmly. "Once in a while I get a bright idea myself." He said then, glancing at his watch, "We'll have to be getting backstage, though, now. Buff wants everyone around in plenty of time."

Pam followed him down the narrow stairway. The old boat was murmurous with sound now, voices and laughter and footsteps as people were ushered to their seats. Many curious, amused glances were cast at Pam and Alan as they made their way along the narrow side deck outside the auditorium. "There are some of the players," Pam heard whispered over and over. And she felt her heat begin to race again with excitement.

As they went through the doorway that led backstage, they came face to face with Geneva Day. She wore the becoming costume of white satin and sequins which she would use in her vaudeville act. The pale blond hair curling against her shoulders in a fashion longer than the prevailing one, was held back by a wide silver band. She looked really lovely, Pam thought. And she'd have said as much, being quite willing to meet Geneva halfway in friendliness, had no the other girl dismissed her with one aloof glance to concentrate her attention warmly on Alan.

"Darling," she drawled in her low-pitched voice, "I've been looking everywhere for you."

She tucked her hand possessively through Alan's arm and drew him off with her, leaving Pam standing alone. Well, all right, Pam thought, resentment warming her cheeks at the other girl's attitude. If that's how you want to be, I don't care!

Geneva Day's friendship and liking weren't vital to her. She had lots of other friends. The thought occurred to Pam that Geneva might be afraid she was trying to get Alan away from her. There was no denying that he had been paying a good deal of attention to Pam, even today after Geneva's arrival. A lot of it was tied up with the play, Pam knew. Still she felt that Alan liked her and she knew in her heart she found him quite attractive.

Pam thought, a demon of mischief prompting her, If Gen doesn't watch out, I might just decide really to go after her precious Alan. After all, she hasn't got him chained to her like an organ grinder's monkey.

In the girls' dressing room all was confusion. The air was thick with powder, fragrant with perfume, electric with tension. Everyone was scrambling over each other for a last reassuring look in the one full-length mirror. Pam checked her costume, too, fluffing her skirts and adjusting her bonnet's bow. She really looked the part of Clarabelle, who, as the program said, was "a lovely, but not too bright heroine." The program resembled an authentic old showboat playbill, but the humorous interpolations after each character's name set the key for the broad spoofing the melodrama was going to get. Of Archibald Sutherland, the part played by Alan, it said, "a villain of hideous proportions." And it described the hero as "Clarabelle's sweetheart, a youth of much virtue, but little intellect." There was also, near the top of the sheet, a note that read: "The members of the audience are EXPRESSLY REQUESTED to follow those most NATURAL INCLINATIONS and INSTINCTS which reward VILLAINY with hisses and disapprobation and *VIRTUE IN DISTRESS* with applause."

Pam smiled a little, just thinking of it. Then there was a knock at the door and, after a moment's discreet wait, Buff stuck his head in to announce, "Overture in five minutes. Everybody ready? Looks as though we're really going to get started on time tonight."

If Buff's words had been a cue, disaster couldn't have struck more instantaneously. Scarcely had he finished speaking when every light on the *Regina* went out.

CHAPTER EIGHT

A SURPRISE FOR PAM

"SOMETIME MAYBE," Tip supposed, biting her fingernail nervously, "we may laugh about this. Remember how we used to hear of such things happening and just think they were terribly funny?"

"But they weren't happening to us," Pam answered.

She pushed against Tip so that she, too, could peer out through the tiny opening in the curtain. The audience was becoming somewhat restive, although the orchestra, playing so manfully in the half-dark, helped to make them forget that the performance was now almost half an hour late in starting. The summer dusk was still bright enough to keep the people from realizing that all the lights had gone off. Unaware that the main generator, which supplied electric power for the *Regina*, was out of commission, they seemed to accept the dimness as the customary thing, and to be quite unconcerned about it. Only the showboaters were aware of the true state of affairs.

From her vantage point on the stage, Pam could glimpse Mike Bradley, one leg over the balcony rail, working feverishly on the big main spotlight that illuminated the stage—or that should illuminate it. All the male members of the showboat crew, many of them incongruously in costume, were working somewhere or other in a concerted effort to get at least the stage lights going again. It had been Mike's brilliant idea that if these could be rigged up to the small generator the ham radio enthusiasts had in their headquarters on the *Dink*, the performance could go on. Then, while it was in progress, there would be time to attempt the necessary repairs on the big main generator. This was the end toward which every pair of available hands was working.

"The dressing-rooms," Pam murmured, "must be like

the Black Hole of Calcutta. How will we ever change costume?"

"I don't care," Tip said fervently. "If they can only get the stage lights going, we'll change by the sense of touch if necessary." She turned to Pam, her eyes wide with a horrified thought. "Wouldn't it be ghastly if we had to refund everybody's money?"

Pam could only nod, as appalled as Tip at the possibility. The *Regina* was supposed to pay her own way and if they had to start off deep in the red, they might not manage to catch up all season. It could mean the end of the showboat course for all time and that would break poor Buff's heart. The showboat was his dream child, his delight. All his work and sweat and planning —why, it just couldn't be spoiled by anything so purely mechanical as a balky generator!

She remembered hearing tales of another time the generator had conked out a couple of seasons before. That had been late in the performance, though, and they had resorted to the makeshift expedient of having the ushers sit in the front of the auditorium, their powerful flashlights trained on the stage. The audience had entered enthusiastically into the spirit of the thing and the show had gone on. But it would be almost impossible to light an entire production that way. And an opening performance, too, when everyone was jittery to start with and none too sure of himself.

As though urged on by Pam's anxious thoughts and those of all the other worried players, the big light Mike had been working on flashed into sudden brilliance. Pam blinked and such a sense of thankfulness surged through her that she actually felt chokey. She and Tip hugged each other and danced about delightedly, just as other exuberant figures were doing all over the shadowy stage. Their collective sigh of relief was drowned out by a brisk spattering of applause from the audience. But the onlookers, Pam realized, were merely applauding because they thought the performance was about to start. They had no idea of how close they had come to not seeing any show at all.

"Mike should take a bow," Pam murmured to Tip elatedly.

Tip nodded, admitting, "He's a very handy guy to have around in an emergency."

Breathless male members of the cast began pouring onto the stage, stumbling a little in the dimness that still lay behind the curtain, wiping their soiled hands on their handkerchiefs. Buff Quinn rushed from the wings and his presence helped to subdue the whispered babel.

"Now we can roll," Buff said exultantly, motioning them all to their places in the opening scene. "We'll rig up flashlights in both dressing rooms and you'll just have to make your changes as best you can. Maybe Cap and Mike can get the big generator going again before too long. But we can't keep the audience waiting any longer. Good luck, kids."

As he moved back toward the wings, Pam saw him lift an arm authoritatively to signal the opening of the curtain.

To Pam's surprise, the play went off very well. She didn't forget any vital lines. She didn't give any of her fellow actors a miscue. Her palms might perspire and her brow feel positively feverish, but she was getting laughs where she was supposed to get laughs, just as the others were. Maybe the failure of the lights had served to take their minds off themselves and their acting sufficiently so that none of them suffered from stage fright or self-consciousness. Maybe the necessity of making costume changes in the still-dark dressing rooms, of checking their make-up by flashlight, left them too limp with laughter to tighten up when they did get on stage. Never had Pam participated in a more relaxed and smooth-running performance.

The audience was wonderful, applauding and hissing, entering into the spirit of the old melodrama for all it was worth. The mere sight of Alan, tossing his long cape dramatically over his shoulder, twisting his black moustache, was enough to bring on an outburst of good-natured boos. The hilarious onlookers kept warning Pam of his evil intentions as he beguiled her into walking with

54

him along the railroad track. And when the great cardboard train, borne from behind by half a dozen perspiring young men, came rushing toward her helpless form, everyone urged the hero on to rescue her with greater dispatch. It was all grand fun and the audience enjoyed it to the full.

And afterwards, one act after another of the vaudeville show was climaxed with an enthusiastic roar of applause.

"Are showboat audiences always like this?" Pam asked Buff as they watched from the wings while Geneva Day danced and sang. She looked too lovely, Pam reflected, to be as unpleasant as she was.

"I think they get a charge out of participating," Buff said and chuckled. "The professional theater takes itself so seriously, I sometimes wonder if the audience doesn't feel a little inhibited. But here they can do everything but climb right up on the stage with the actors—and they love it!" He told Pam, then, "You were great tonight. I'm proud of you. Not everyone could have done so well on such short notice."

Pam felt a warm rush of pleasure at the compliment. As she thanked the professor, she realized that this was a part of the reason for his great popularity. He was hard to please, unless one did one's best. But he was also quick with a word of praise when he felt it to be deserved.

The rest of the lights still weren't on when the show was over. Mike had made a hasty trip in to town and secured a new part for the balky generator. The captain and he and some of the others were still toiling over it, but their efforts had not as yet been successful. Buff went on stage and made a short curtain speech, explaining to the audience the makeshift system that had been used for lighting the play. He thanked the crowd for its enthusiasm and said that ushers with flashlights were stationed at the stairways and other danger points to see that everyone got off the boat without mishap.

When this feat had been accomplished some fifteen minutes later and the still good-natured crowd was safe on shore, all the showboat crew felt a sense of happy relief. Buff went off to suggest to the grimy, perspiring workers that they let the generator wait till morning, when they could see better and wouldn't be so tired. And the cast began scattering to get out of costume.

Alan, already changed into slacks and sport shirt, caught Pam's arm and detained her for a moment as she and several other girls headed for the dressing room.

"You were terrific!" He added his commendation to all the rest Pam had received, but somehow, coming from Alan, it made her heart lift and race.

"Not as terrific as you," Pam told him, "but thanks." It was true, she thought. Alan was a natural on the stage. He had the audience with him from his first line.

His hand tightened on her elbow. "I'll see you later in the dining cabin. Aunt Lucy's managed to fix our opening night snack. But we'll have to eat it by candlelight."

"That should be fun." Pam smiled and turned away.

A late supper on the opening night of each new play was an old showboat custom, she knew. But would she really get to see Alan at close enough range for conversation, or would Geneva contrive to keep him all to herself?

"I'll bet she'll try," Pam murmured under her breath as she quickly creamed away her make-up in the eerie, crowded semidarkness of the noisy dressing room. Propped-up flashlights cast grotesque shadows on the walls as girls struggled out of their costumes and into regular clothes.

Pam was dressed first of all, spurred on by the hope that if she could get to the dining cabin before Geneva, she might be able to thwart the other girl's designs on Alan. It would serve her right, Pam thought, recalling the slighting way Geneva had treated her earlier in the evening. Resentment flared anew at the memory.

She slipped out of the dressing room quietly and onto the narrow sidedeck. Moonlight silhouetted a tall, broad shouldered form leaning on the rail in an attitude of waiting. Pam's breath caught in surprise as the figure straightened. She couldn't see his face, but she was almost certain of his identity just the same. "Alan?" she moved toward him.

"Afraid not," a rather drawling, familiar voice said quietly.

But it wasn't a voice Pam expected to hear at this time or place. Nor was the smiling face her eyes strained to make out one she was remotely expecting to see.

"Jeff!" she gasped incredulously, scarcely able to speak for the shaken hammering of her heart. "Oh, Jeff!" But how could it be Jeff, she asked herself? It just wasn't possible!

"Hi, honey." Pam felt his big hands clasp hers hard and knew this was no creature of her imagination. His nearness drove all thoughts of Alan from her mind.

"But how—but when—" her voice sounded high-pitched, unnatural in her own ears. She got it under a little better control as k, "Have you been here all evening, all during the play "

"Sure was," Jeff drawled. "I only missed a few minutes at the beginning. I'd have been on time, but I had a flat. You were having so much trouble with the lights, though, I figured I'd better wait till the play was over to let you know I was here. I didn't want to stir you up any more."

"You drove all that way?" Pam murmured. "It's a hundred miles, isn't it?"

"Eighty-seven to be exact." Jeff chuckled. "Only a couple of hours if I hadn't been delayed." His hands tightened on hers and Pam thrilled to his touch. Now that they were together again, she realized fully how much she'd missed him. Even as busy as she'd been, as absorbed in the newness and strangeness of showboat life, there had been moments when she had ached with a queer little sense of emptiness, of loss. Now that Jeff was here, her delight in his presence crowded her heart.

"But—how did you know I'd be playing the lead?" She was still groping for the cause of his unexpected visit. She hadn't had time to write and tell him. No one had.

"I didn't," Jeff told her. Pam's eyes, more accustomed

now to the moonlight, could see his grin plainly. "I just came to see you. Period. I knew it was opening night, of course. But I didn't care what size part you had. It was just an extra kick to find you were the leading lady. Honey, I'm real proud of you."

He bent his head and Pam lifted her lips. It was a quick kiss, since she knew that girls would be spilling out of the dressing room onto the deck any moment. But she felt the impact of it right down to her heels just the same.

And Jeff's voice was husky, a little unsteady, murmuring, "That's what I came for, if you want to know. Gee, I've missed you."

"It seems like months, doesn't it?" Pam whispered. And yet only a couple of weeks had elapsed since they'd been seeing each other practically every day at college. Now that he was here, his arms about her real and solid, she couldn't bear the thought of having him go. She coaxed, "You can stay overnight, can't you, Jeff? I'm sure the fellows can squeeze you into the Man Hole if—"

But he was shaking his head firmly in the negative, just as Pam had been desolately sure he would. "I'll have to get back tonight. The folks are expecting me and I've got work to do tomorrow morning."

"You and your old farmwork!" Pam exclaimed, knowing she was being unreasonable and not caring. Disappointment ached in her throat.

"Why waste time arguing about things that can't be helped, honey?" Jeff's hand was soothing on her shoulder, his voice gentle.

Pam felt her momentary flash of anger die. Jeff was sensible and mature, not prone to follow crazy, spur-of-the-moment impulses. Was it because he was a little older, because he'd already had to face the stark reality of army life, because his farm background had tended to make him think things through and then follow the decisions he'd reached? Or was it that Jeff himself was different, a stronger, more solid character than the other

58

men Pam knew? Except possibly Mike, she thought. In many respects Mike and Jeff were a lot alike.

Aloud she said rather forlornly, "But you'll want to see Mike and Penny, won't you? Can't you stay long enough to have supper with us? We can go up to the dining cabin now. Everyone will be getting together there."

"Okay." Jeff let himself be persuaded. "I'd like that. Only let's detour around the deck a little first. After all, it was mainly you I came to see."

Pam tucked her hand through his arm as they moved off. She laid her cheek against his shoulder, liking the feel of it.

"Glad I came?" Jeff asked.

Pam nodded. "It makes tonight just perfect."

She meant what she said. But even with the words on her lips she was aware of the thought of Alan stealing slyly back into her mind. Would the fact that Jeff had come all this way to see her make her seem more desirable to Alan, she wondered? Not that his opinion was important to her. Let Geneva have him. Pam had Jeff and he was all she wanted.

And yet, she asked herself, why was it that any man she was unsure of always exerted a perverse sort of fascination for her?

CHAPTER NINE

A QUARREL AND A QUESTION

BY THE TIME Pam and Jeff reached the dining cabin, everyone else was assembled there. Candlelight fell softly over the long buffet table, spread generously with the rapidly disappearing sandwiches and cookies and soft drinks Aunt Lucy had prepared despite the handicap of darkness. She was hovering about, beaming and seeing to it that all of them got plenty to eat. This was always one of Aunt Lucy's main concerns. Captain Anderson, a half-eaten sandwich in one hand, waved it to emphasize the point he was making about how careful they must be with candles on the showboat.

"Fire was the scourge of the rivers in the old days," he declaimed. "I've seen boats burn right down to the water line because someone got careless and upset an oil lamp. Now these candles," he gestured toward the table, "I wouldn't leave 'em unwatched for a minute. People get too cocky about fire. That's why we won't let the audience smoke even during intermission unless they go clear ashore. 'Course it's different with us people who live aboard and have got enough sense to be cautious." He grinned over at Buff, who was lighting a cigarette at that moment and patted his own shirt pocket, from which the stem of his pipe protruded.

Then someone caught sight of Jeff, standing just inside the door with Pam, and cries of welcome and pleased surprise exploded around the room. In a moment the two late arrivals were the center of a lively group.

Mike hurried up to clap Jeff on the shoulder. "You old so-and-so, it's great to see you! Penny told me you were here, but we were afraid you'd left without seeing anyone but Pam."

"Now you ought to know I wouldn't do that." Jeff grinned.

"You knew he was here," Pam accused Penny, with a little laugh, "and didn't tell me?"

"He said he wanted to surprise you," Penny explained. "I couldn't spoil it all just because I happened to be the usher who showed him to his seat."

Her eyes met Pam's in a deep look of understanding. She knew how much Jeff's visit meant to her twin, how strong was the attraction between them. Both Penny and Mike hoped that in Jeff, Pam had found the man who could hold her for all time. Pam sensed this desire on their part and resented it just a little. After all, falling in love was her own affair. Maybe she had been fickle in the past. Still, a girl had to be sure, didn't she? And although she knew what a grand person Jeff was, although she was so fond of him, there was still a doubt,

60

hovering like a faint shadow, in Pam's mind. She wanted
to be sure, just as Jeff did, that the feeling between them
was real and lasting. He didn't want her to make up her
mind in a hurry.

Many of the showboaters knew Jeff. Pam was aware
of a little inner glow of pride as she moved about the big
room, introducing him to those who didn't. There was
no denying he was good-looking in a rugged masculine
way. His hazel eyes crinkled half-shut when he smiled.
Beneath his close-cut brown hair his skin was tanned
almost Indian-dark. And he had a pleasant easygoing
manner that drew people to him.

"You look," Geneva Day said as she smiled up into
Jeff's eyes after acknowledging Pam's introduction, "as
though you've been spending your time lying around on
the beach."

She's really beautiful, Pam thought unwillingly.

Geneva's pale hair curled softly against her bare shoulders. A deceptively simple aqua cotton dress with a
deep-scooped neckline matched her eyes perfectly and
had probably cost as much as any six dresses in the
room, Pam realized.

Jeff chuckled, correcting, "You're wrong there. I've
been riding around on a tractor. But I guess the effect's
much the same when it comes to getting tanned."

"Are you a farmer?" Geneva asked. She had one hand
tucked closely through Alan Richmond's arm. Pam
couldn't quite decide whether he liked having her hand
there. His dark glance met Pam's in a look the meaning
of which she wasn't sure.

"That I am," Jeff told Geneva. He turned his full
attention to Pam once more, asking, "Shall we get our-
selves a sandwich? I'll have to be shoving off before
long."

Did she imagine the slightly amused, superior quirk of
Geneva's lips, Pam wondered? Geneva was just snob-
bish enough to take that attitude toward farmers. Moving over to the buffet table with Jeff, Pam sought to
dismiss the other girl from her mind. She tried to dismiss Alan, too. Let him stay tied to Geneva by the

61

slender deceptive strength of that hand on his arm, the undeniable pull of her beauty. Pam didn't care. Why should she?

Later, when Jeff was about to leave, he and Pam lingered for a few moments alone in the dim quiet of the deserted foredeck.

Jeff asked, his lips close to Pam's ear, his arm about her, "You like it here, don't you? It's all as much fun as you expected?"

"Oh, yes!" Pam told him. "It's wonderful. I love it."

"Good!" he said.

But something in his tone made Pam assure him quickly, "I miss you, though, Jeff. Really I do."

He kissed her, his lips hard on hers, and Pam's arms locked about his neck holding him to her. If only this moment could go on forever, if only he didn't have to leave—

Jeff said huskily, "Just don't go getting interested in any other guys. I saw the way Richmond looked at you."

"Geneva's got her personal 'Hands Off' sign hung on him," Pam said. "Didn't you notice?"

"Yeah." Jeff's tone was dry. "But I'm not sure you can read."

"I can," Pam told him. "You needn't go issuing ultimatums."

"I don't mean to do that ever," Jeff said solemnly. "If I sound like it, you tell me off. You're free. We're both free. I know how I feel, but it's no good unless you're sure, too. That's what this summer's for, so you can be sure. Am I making sense?"

"You're sounding—awfully serious." There was a breathless little break in Pam's voice.

Somewhere far down the river a foghorn mourned. She shivered at the melancholy sound and Jeff's arm tightened about her.

He complained ruefully, "The trouble is, you're such a baby. Why couldn't I have picked myself a girl my own age?"

Pam leaned her head against his shoulder. "You're only two years older than I," she reminded. But that was in years, she knew. Actually Jeff was much more mature than she in judgment and outlook.

"Almost three," he corrected. "If I hadn't gone into the Marines, I'd have been practically through school instead of just starting. As it is, with three more years of college ahead of me, and having to live at home and help with the farm, it'll be a long time before I'll be in a position to talk seriously to a girl. So," his tone grew philosophical, "we won't talk seriously. We'll just go on trifling with each other's affections." He reached out to smooth a silky curl of dark hair back from Pam's cheek, his big hand very gentle.

For a moment, Pam thought, he had sounded as though he were on the verge of a proposal. She wasn't quite sure whether she was glad or sorry he'd backed away from it. In a way she wanted him to go on and say in so many words that he loved her, to ask her to marry him later on. But in another way she'd rather have things continue as they were. She was young and having a wonderful summer. There would be plenty of time later on to make up her mind about so serious a matter as marriage.

"It's late," Jeff said regretfully. "I've got to go."

"Will you be back soon?" Pam coaxed, the hurt of parting beginning to ache in her throat.

"Not too soon," Jeff shook his head. "It's kind of hard for me to get away. Dad's not well at all. His heart's been acting up and he has to take things awfully easy."

"I'm sorry," Pam said.

She liked Jeff's family, his father with his keen, intelligent weathered face, his mother, white-haired and vital, his married sister and the younger brother and sister who were children still.

Jeff held her close and kissed her. Then with no further word, he lifted his hand in a little gesture of farewell and strode off down the gangplank. Watching him go, Pam felt like crying. She drew a deep shaken breath. So long as his kiss stirred her so much, that was enough for now. . . .

When she slipped into the Hen Roost, most of the bunks were already occupied. Not everyone was sleeping, though. There was an occasional buzz of conversation about the big shadowed room. Tip Flanders, who was just climbing into her bunk, motioned toward the flashlight that was propped up on one of the dressers.

"Leave it on," she told Pam. "Not all the kids are in yet."

"Okay." Pam started getting ready for bed.

As Tip wriggled under the covers of her bunk, she asked Pam, her tone impishly teasing. "Were the farewells tender?"

"What do you think?" Pam's answer was good-humoredly casual.

"I'd hate to break away if he were mine," Carla Trent admitted from across the room. "Those muscles!"

"He is quite a guy," Tip agreed, "that is, in looks and personality. If only he had some other occupation. Can you imagine Pam on a farm?"

"Pipe down," someone growled from an upper bunk. "I'm dead."

Someone else yawned audibly and bed springs squeaked.

As she passed Penny's bunk on her way to her own, she paused a moment. Penny raised herself on one elbow and the moonlight fell full on her face, revealing the question in her eyes. If they had been at home, or even at college, where their rooms adjoined, Pam could have succumbed to the urge she felt to confide in Penny. They always talked things over after they went to bed. It was a custom that dated clear back to their childhood. But how could you talk over personal matters here, with a dozen girls in the same room? If they were asleep you'd waken them. If they were awake, they'd naturally listen in. Pam smiled down at Penny and shrugged her shoulders. And Penny nodded in understanding. Confidences would have to wait until they had some measure of privacy.

All Pam could do was murmur, for her sister's ears alone, "Everything's fine, Pen. 'Night."

Penny reached out and gave Pam's fingers a little squeeze as she answered, " 'Night."

Pam stretched out in her own bunk and lay there, arms crossed behind her head, eyes fixed on space, thinking about Jeff. Memories of the performance crowded in on her, too, the wonderful things Buff and the others had said to her, the remembered thrill of applause. Still Jeff remained uppermost in her thoughts. His visit overshadowed all the rest of the wonderful evening.

Someone turned over to demand, "Why can't we turn off that darned flashlight? It shines in my eyes. Who's still out anyway?"

"Gen Day," Tip's voice supplied.

Another girl yawned, "And Maggie Turner."

"I'm back!" Maggie, slim and blond, her face animated with excitement, came hurrying in. "But I don't know when Gen will be. She and Alan are having a terrific scrap. Tom and I could hear them as we came along the other side of the deck. A fight like that won't get patched up in a hurry."

Interested voices began firing questions at Maggie. What were Geneva and Alan fighting about? What were they saying?

"How would I know?" Maggie asked innocently. "You don't think I'd stoop to eavesdropping? I could just tell by their tones that they weren't billing and cooing."

She had been getting into her pajamas and now she asked, her hand poised above the flashlight, "Shall I douse it?"

"Yes!" several voices exclaimed. And a couple of others added plaintive requests that everybody shut up and go to sleep.

"Maybe," Tip Flanders commented hopefully as pitch darkness prevailed at last, "if Gen and Alan give each other the air, some of the rest of us will have a chance with him. She's sure hung onto him ever since she came aboard."

"Shhhhh . . ."

The Hen Roost was quiet finally. Still Geneva hadn't come in. Were she and Alan breaking up for good, Pam wondered? And if they did, would Alan's interest turn toward her? She lay there, her thoughts darting restlessly between Jeff and Alan, disturbed at her own indecision. Were other girls torn like this, unsure of their own hearts? Penny wasn't, Pam knew. Penny had known Mike was the man she wanted almost from their first meeting. And Mike was equally certain about his feeling toward her. Lucky Penny, Pam thought, to be so sensible. She felt unstable as a weather vane, turning this way and that, first toward Jeff, then Alan.

And what of Geneva? Pam asked herself. She wouldn't give up easily, especially if she sensed Alan might be growing interested in the girl she disliked. Maybe that was what they were quarreling about—but the mere fact that they were quarreling didn't mean the end of things for them. Lots of quarrels were made up. Even if Geneva didn't want him, she might try to hang onto Alan just to thwart Pam.

Jeff, Jeff, Pam's heart cried. Why can't you be here all the time? When we're together, I'm so sure it's you I want. But when you're gone and Alan's here, I'm not positive.

She wasn't even sure whether her own interest in Alan was real or whether it grew out of an urge on her part to put Geneva in her place, to show her she wasn't so completely irresistible as she seemed to think.

Finally, Pam was able to put it all out of her mind sufficiently so that she fell asleep.

Something awakened her and she didn't know whether she'd been sleeping hours or minutes. The Hen Roost was very dark and still. And yet there had been some faint sound—Pam strained her ears to hear if it were repeated. At last it came again, a low sob smothered by a pillow almost to inaudibility. Yet someone was crying quietly in the darkness, she was sure of it.

Was it Geneva, Pam wondered, or merely someone suffering the pangs of homesickness? There was no way she could be sure without intruding on someone else's privacy. And that she wouldn't do.

She lay very stiff and still in her bunk, listening and

wondering. And at last the sound of crying died away into silence. But it took quite a long while for Pam to fall asleep again.

CHAPTER TEN

FEUD

AS THE DAYS ON THE *Regina* followed one another, each filled to overflowing with work and play and climaxed with the excitement of putting on a show every night, the memory of that unidentifiable weeping dimmed in Pam's mind. It remained an unsolved mystery, but its importance was questionable. Some of the girls who hadn't been away from home so long before were prone to spells of homesickness. It might have been one of them Pam heard. If it had been Geneva, certainly her eyes showed no trace of redness the next morning. Nor did her arrogant self-confidence seem lessened. Her relationship with Alan continued much the same, despite their reported quarrel. They were still friends, who saw a good deal of each other. If Alan chafed at Geneva's possessive attitude, the only evidence of his resentment was the fact that he spent some of his free time with Pam. Nor did Pam do anything to discourage his attentions.

Penny couldn't understand her twin's attitude. She said as much during one of their infrequent moments of privacy. The two of them had the galley all to themselves one morning as they peeled a small mountain of boiled potatoes for salad. And Penny took advantage of her chance to tell Pam, her gray eyes troubled, "Mike and I were discussing Alan Richmond last night. We decided he's the type of egotist who gets a charge out of having a couple of girls at swords' points over him. He's leading you both on, Pam. Can't you see that?"

Pam smiled reassuringly at her twin. "I don't think much of you and Mike as a pair of amateur psychologists. But I appreciate your concern in my behalf. Are you afraid I'm a poor little helpless moth, fluttering closer and closer to the deadly flame of Alan's irresistible attraction?"

"No, of course not," Penny said. "It's just that—well, he's building up more bad feeling between you and Geneva all the time. And there was plenty to start with. Not that it's your fault. She hasn't been nice to you, I know."

"An understatement if I ever heard one," Pam said tartly. "She's snubbed me and belittled me and tried to push me around generally. I don't have to take that from anyone. I think I've been quite forbearing, all things considered."

"I know." Penny cut a little spot out of the potato she was paring with clinical care. "But it isn't helping the situation any for you to encourage Alan. Especially when you aren't even very interested in him." Penny's questioning glance lifted to her twin's face. "You're not really interested in him, are you?"

Pam shrugged lightly. "He's attractive and fun to be with. He seems to like me and I like him. And he's not Geneva's private property, you know. He has a mind of his own and if he chooses to pay some attention to me, I don't see why I should run and hide."

Penny was silent for a moment, a little frown between her brows.

"Don't worry," Pam told her. "I can take care of myself." In a way, she thought, it was funny for Penny to be giving her advice in a situation of this sort. She had always had more dates than Penny, more young men clamoring for her favor. Penny was content with Mike, he was the only serious beau she'd ever had, or probably ever would have. Pam had always been able to wrap most men around her little finger. Except Jeff. Jeff had a mind of his own, even if he was in love with her. Maybe it was Jeff Penny was really worried about, or the effect on Jeff of Pam's interest in Alan. Pam asked, "Are you afraid I may get to like Alan more than Jeff?"

Penny said firmly, "I give you credit for more sense

than that. Jeff's worth ten of Alan and I think you know it."

Pam told her, "Jeff wants me to have this summer free of any restrictions. We've got things to think through, Jeff and I, things to decide later on. But he won't care if I have a little fun with Alan. There's no harm in that."

"I know." Penny nodded. "But it can make more trouble between you and Geneva and it just doesn't seem worth it. Buff won't put up with a regular feud developing. We've all got to get along together."

"Don't worry about Buff," Pam murmured. She felt a little shield of resistance rise between her and Penny. "Geneva and I are quite decent to each other when he's around. But I won't let her walk all over me at other times, just to keep peace!"

Penny laid her hand appealingly on Pam's arm, a little apologetic smile curving her lips. "Of course, I don't expect you to do that. You know I'm on your side, Pam. But if you'll just try—"

"Geneva can try, too," Pam cut in shortly.

Still, the memory of Penny's words lingered in her mind, unwilling as she was to heed them. Penny's advice was sensible, Pam knew. Yet why should she make all the concessions? If Geneva showed any inclination toward friendliness, Pam would try to meet her halfway. She was well aware of how annoyed Buff would be with both of them if he realized their continuing enmity. And it would be impossible to keep the situation from his notice indefinitely. Buff was too observant for that. And the showboat was too small a world to contain bitter resentments, rivalries that carried within themselves the seeds of further trouble. But it was also too small for Pam to let Geneva triumph over her, while everyone looked on and saw what was happening. Pam's own pride stopped her from discouraging Alan's attentions, just so Geneva might be placated.

It was only natural that there should be a lot of talk about home around the Hen Roost. Each girl spoke of her family often and whenever she received a letter she told of things that were happening at home, related what her parents and sisters and brothers were doing. Everyone knew a good deal about everyone else's background. The fact that Pam's and Penny's mother was on her honeymoon, that they had a brand-new stepfather, was common knowledge. Everyone knew that Tip Flanders had a brother in the air force and that her father was a lawyer, that Ellen Carr was an only child, that Carla Trent's parents were both artists employed by rival advertising agencies. But they knew most of all about Geneva Day's family, because Geneva was forever talking about them. There was her mother, Elissa, who was so beautiful she had been offered contracts by several movie studios. Only, of course, she wasn't interested, because she was far too happy and contented just being a wife and a mother to think of taking on a career. Geneva's father was a highly successful banker, with a whole chain of banks under his control. But he didn't have to work at his job very hard, because the banks had been founded by his father and Uncle Andy and they were an institution all up and down the West Coast. So Geneva's father, whom she called Curt in the modern casual manner, spent a lot of his time playing polo, which was his favorite hobby. And he and Geneva's mother were still madly in love, and were both almost embarrassingly devoted to Geneva.

"I never thought they'd give in and let me spend this summer on the showboat," Geneva said with an indulgent little smile. "They kept thinking up reasons to detain me, like that terrific party they threw for Uncle Andy, which made me so late in getting here. I think they felt if they could keep me at home long enough, I might change my mind about coming out here at all. But I'd given my word."

Pam flashed Penny an unobtrusive look that said, "Too bad they couldn't dissuade her." And a faint smile twitched Penny's lips.

Geneva often dropped seemingly casual little remarks which, added together, gave quite a fabulous picture of her family's estate in Santa Monica. No one could remain ignorant of the fact that it had a swimming pool, a corps of servants and a guest list that included a great many famous and wealthy people.

"I don't see how she ever tore herself away," Pam confided to Tip once after a larger than usual dose of Geneva's reminiscences. "Those doting parents lavishing all their attention on her, that glittering social life—and then to give it all up to spend a summer on an old tub like the *Regina* with us poor peasants!"

Tip laughed. "She does spread it on, doesn't she? I wonder if she actually knows all those movie stars, or if she's just bragging?"

Pam shrugged. "Even if she does know them she doesn't have to be forever dragging them into the conversation. Or am I just being catty because I don't like her?"

Tip shook her head. "She rubs me the wrong way, too, and a lot of the other kids. Of course, some of them are impressed."

Pam said analytically, "She's really beautiful and quite talented. But she has one of the most egotistical, unpleasant personalities I've ever run into."

"That's putting it mildly," Tip agreed. And she added, with a perverse little grin, "It'll serve her right if you get Alan away from her."

"Alan's a free agent," Pam said. "But Geneva acts as if she owns him. No wonder it makes him sore. Just because they went around together for a while at school doesn't mean she can hang onto him forever. I'm not deliberately trying to take him away from her. But I'm not going to let him think I don't enjoy his company, because I do."

"Atta girl!" Tip approved. "If I can't get him myself, I can enjoy seeing you take Gen down a peg. . . ."

For a week the showboat troupe played *Virtue Rewarded* to full houses. Then, because of previous commitments, they planned to move on upriver to the next town on their itinerary.

"If we leave them wanting more," Buff pointed out, "they'll be watching eagerly for the *Regina* next season."

71

He spoke with the assurance of several years' experience.

Captain Anderson nodded his white head in sage agreement. "It used to be differ'nt in the old days. Then these river towns never got no other entertainment. They were hungry to see a show. Now with movies and tee-vee and all, it's a wonder they turn out for us as well as they do."

"We're an anachronism." Buff grinned. "It's partly the novelty that draws them. But that wears off if we stay too long."

The day the showboat lifted anchor, almost everyone arose at dawn in order not to miss anything. Pam and Penny joined the yawning crowd that assembled, shivering, on deck in the sharp damp chill of early morning. Mike and a few other boys were busy helping Captain Anderson get the boat under way. But most of the troupe were cast in the role of onlookers at this skilled operation. The sun was just rising and in its pink glow the river mists drifted like opalescent veils across the face of the water, gradually fading. There was an almost dreamlike quality of unreality about the scene.

"Isn't it beautiful?" Penny said softly, her eyes wide with appreciation.

Pam nodded, as touched as her twin by the eerie loveliness of the morning. "It reminds me of one of those movies where they dance on clouds."

"Such a poetic thought at an hour like this!" Alan Richmond's growl close beside her startled Pam and made her smile. "I should have stayed in bed." He yawned widely.

"Why didn't you?" Pam asked.

Alan grinned, admitting, "I had a hunch you'd be up. Can't think of another good reason."

"Look!" Penny exclaimed wonderingly. "We're moving!"

"Wasn't that the whole idea?" Alan asked.

But Pam's glance followed that of her twin, ignoring his sarcasm. Sure enough, the *Regina* was in motion. It seemed strange that this should be so, although the sound of the *Dink's* diesel motor was clearly audible in the dawn stillness. But living on the showboat as they did, going

72

down the gangplank to the shore dozens of times a day, it was easy to fall into the habit of thinking of the boat as something fixed and stationary.

Penny hurried over to the rail for a better view of the shore line slipping slowly by. Pam and Alan were left standing alone. A glance at the others on the upper deck showed Pam that Geneva wasn't around.

She asked, her smile faintly teasing, "Where's Geneva?"

Alan shrugged. "Sleeping, no doubt. Don't you know her well enough to realize it would take more than the boat raising anchor to get her up any earlier than usual?"

Pam said, "I don't know her well at all and both of us are quite happy to keep it that way."

Alan chuckled. "Why have you got it in for each other so?"

"Ask her." Pam's chin lifted.

"I'd rather ask you," Alan told her. "Is it because she's still mad over your getting the lead when she thought she had it cinched? Or is there more to it than that?"

"Let's just say we're not very congenial," Pam suggested, "and leave it at that."

But Alan wasn't content to leave it. "Have I anything to do with it?" he pressed. His hand moved down Pam's arm to clasp hers. Would he have done that, she wondered, if Geneva had been around to see?

She tried to withdraw her fingers, then stopped as Alan's grip tightened. "Have I?" he repeated.

Pam said, keeping her tone light but unable to ignore the quickened beating of her heart, "Geneva wouldn't like this. You'd better be careful."

"She hasn't a thing to say about my actions." There was a note of determination in Alan's voice. "Don't you know that?"

"I don't think she does," Pam said.

"Then she'll have to learn." Alan's tone was firm. "I still have the right to choose my friends, whatever Gen thinks."

"Sounds like a declaration of independence."

73

"I guess it is," Alan said, grinning. "So—how about a date tonight?"

"A date?" Pam's brows lifted. "Tonight?"

"Sure," Alan said, "why not? We'll be in a brand-new town and we won't be starting performances until day after tomorrow. So let's take advantage of the chance to do a little exploring. We can have dinner off the boat for a change, see a movie. Maybe if we're lucky there might even be someplace to dance."

"Sounds like fun," Pam admitted. "Let's."

She wasn't sure which she got the biggest bang out of, the thought of a real date with Alan, or the realiza~'on of the effect it would undoubtedly have on Geneva.

CHAPTER ELEVEN

SCENE IN A POST OFFICE

CAPTAIN ANDERSON, WHO KNEW every bend of the Ohio, manipulated the big wheel in the pilothouse during their trip upriver. Mike was kept busy operating the *Dink*. The only other boats they encountered on the whole trip were a couple of coal barges, slipping silently along with their black cargo through the morning mists.

"It must have been exciting in the old days," Pam remarked as she leaned her elbows on the rail between Alan and Penny.

"Steamboat round the bend and all that Mark Twain sort of stuff?" Alan grinned.

"And those races they used to have between boats," Penny put in, her eyes shining. "The *Robert E. Lee*—wasn't that the one that was so famous?"

Pam nodded. "And think of the river-boat gamblers, with their sideburns and ruffled shirt cuffs."

"All the better for concealing stray aces," Alan supplied drily. "But if anyone accused them of cheating, they had to fight a duel to uphold their honor."

"Weren't they mostly on the Mississippi, though?" Penny queried.

"I guess so," Pam admitted. "But Cap claims the Ohio was always the main showboat river, because there are so many more towns along it, where the shows could draw big crowds."

"Just like us." Alan chuckled. "We hope!"

It was still morning when the *Dink*, bustling and puffing like a very small mother with a very large child, finally eased the *Regina* into her new berth at River City. Buff Quinn's assistant, Bob Sinclair, had driven on ahead in the station wagon, to take care of getting all the permits and licenses that must be secured before the showboat could dock in a new location. He was the first to come up the gangplank, cheerfully waving a fistful of official-looking documents.

"We're all legal now," he announced. "More red tape! I wonder if it used to be simpler when showboats weren't so rare? Now they look at me as if I'm out of my mind and then start delving into ancient archives to check up on just how much they can stick us." He handed the papers to Buff one by one, enumerating, "Docking permit, license to put on a public performance, permission to connect up with the town's water supply—oh, and I made arrangements for showers at the Y. We can keep clean, too."

The excitement of being in a different town was bubbling in everyone. Buff announced understandingly that when they had finished the jobs already assigned to them, they could have the rest of the day and evening to themselves. Immediately all of them began making plans to explore the town and get acquainted with their new surroundings.

Penny urged Pam, "Come along with Mike and me. We thought we'd go exploring, then eat off the boat just for a change and maybe see a movie if there's anything good showing."

"Thanks," Pam told her, "but I've got a date with Alan. We sort of had the same idea about what we'd do."

"Couldn't we all go together?" Penny suggested. "Unless—" she hesitated a second, her glance questioning, "you'd rather not."

"It sounds like fun," Pam agreed, nodding. Penny and Mike were both good company. She wasn't sure Alan would be so keen on the idea of a double date. But it appealed to her. And why should she let Alan get the idea she was eager to be alone with him? He was self-confident enough as it was.

Actually, he offered no objection when Pam told him of the arrangement she'd made with her twin. "Okay with me," was his comment.

Pam couldn't help being a little curious as to what had transpired between him and Geneva. Had they quarreled again, she won ered? Or did Alan simply feel, as he had said earlier, at he had a right to date any girl he chose? There wa no question in Pam's mind, though, about Geneva's rese tment. The look the other girl gave her, as Pam and Alan followed Penny and Mike gaily down the gangpla k, was like a stab of blue fire.

River City was ld and somewhat dilapidated, sprawling untidily up the hill from the water and spreading out over a considerable area. The business section was a conglomeration of old and new structures, elbowing each other, with the old so reatly predominating that they made the more modern buildings seem out of place. Through distant trees, the were glimpses of stately of lared houses on the hills bove the town.

"Cap was telling me," Mike remarked, "how much more prosperous all thes river towns used to be. That was when boats were the main means of transportation, before the railroads came in."

"Now it's air transportation that's undermining the railroads," Alan put in. "I suppose progress always hurts somebody."

The four of them tramped about cheerfully, up one street and down another, interested in all they saw. They window-shopped and ambled through several stores. They had Cokes in an old drugstore with an ornate marble fountain that had probably been in use for fifty years. They admired well-kept residences, set in the midst of

76

shady lawns, and felt pity for the dwellers in rickety shacks with patched broken windows and tar-paper roofs. And they stopped of one accord, to watch in wide-eyed interest at the open door of a blacksmith shop, where the smith in a stained leather apron was actually shoeing a patient horse.

Alan seemed to enjoy their jaunt as much as the rest of them did. But Pam couldn't help wondering whether, if the two of them had been alone, he would have chosen to do something more glamorous and sophisticated. Perhaps he would have suggested a drink in the lounge of the town's largest and most impressive hotel, instead of having a Coke in a drugstore. Or he might have preferred to eat dinner somewhere other than the picturesque little riverside restaurant they picked because the smell of frying fish tickled their appetites and the place looked clean and inexpensive. This latter consideration was important to Mike, Pam knew. But Alan probably didn't care how much he spent. At least, his attitude always implied he had plenty of money.

Their French fried shrimps were crisp and delicious and the generous wooden bowls of salad were a perfect complement for the rest of the meal. And while they ate, lights started winking on in the gray dusk beyond the windows, like fireflies caught in a net of gauze. Afterwards, sitting in the dark of the town's largest movie, Pam felt Alan's fingers capture hers and close around them firmly. She made no effort to draw her hand away. They sat there, relaxed and easy in the comfortable seats, their shoulders touching, a warmth of liking and congeniality wrapping them about. All in all, it had been a wonderful afternoon and evening, a chance for her and Alan to get much better acquainted than they had been able to on the showboat, under the influence of Geneva's watchfully restraining eye. Pam pushed the thought of the other girl quickly out of her mind. Why let the hampering influence of Geneva intrude on what might develop into a very pleasant relationship?

Life snapped back to regular showboat routine the

next morning—the breakfast bell ringing early; the work sheet to be consulted; jobs to be done. Pam, down on her knees in faded blue jeans and an old tee-shirt, scrubbed the galley floor. But her thoughts were so busy with memories of the evening before, with anticipation of the rehearsals for a new play which were due to start that afternoon, that the job didn't seem too bad. There would be only three more performances of *Virtue Rewarded*. Then the new play would open and run through the following week in River City and for a few days after the *Regina* had moved on to her next scheduled stop. This was customary procedure, Pam had learned—one play running, another being rehearsed, then perhaps a repeat run of the earlier play, but with a changed cast. In this way all the students had a chance to appear in something during the season. Three or possibly four plays in all would be put on and repeated. And there were always new vaudeville routines being dreamed up in the fertile minds of the showboaters. These had to be worked out and rehearsed until they met with Buff's approval. Then they were added to the showboat repertoire, giving it a quality of change and flexibility and keeping the performers from getting into a rut.

Pam's role in the next play was a very small one. But she didn't care. That was the way things went on the *Regina*, a part of the give-and-take that made everyone feel equally important.

"One week a star, the next a walk-on," was Buff's dry commentary. "That way no one develops delusions of grandeur."

Penny would have a part in the new play, too, and Pam was pleased over that. And the two of them were practicing a sister singing-and-dancing act for the vaudeville show. Buff liked the routine they'd worked out and had said he'd use it when they got the rough edges smoothed off.

So distant were Pam's thoughts that she had her unpleasant job done almost before she realized it. The next thing on her schedule was a trip to town with Carla Trent. The two of them had been delegated to call at the local radio station and try to wangle some free time for showboat promotion. This was not too tough an assignment, since interviews with showboat players usually appealed to most small radio outlets.

The River City station proved no exception in this respect. Two pretty, vivacious girls in crisp summer dresses made a most pleasing impression in its rather dim and musty headquarters. The shirt-sleeved middle-aged man who had charge seemed almost dazzled by the unexpected apparition. Before Pam and Carla left they had tactfully let themselves be persuaded to appear on a show the next day. And they had set up interviews for Buff and Captain Anderson and assorted members of the showboat cast.

Carla chuckled as they emerged into the street once more. "He was so co-operative we'll hardly have to do any paid advertising at all. Won't Buff be pleased?"

"He'd better be," Pam said and smiled. "With all the radio time they promised us, everybody in River City ought to hear about the show before we open."

As they turned to head back toward the showboat, a gray brick building across the street caught Pam's eye. "Look," she indicated it to Carla, "there's the post office. Let's see if we've got any mail."

Everyone had supplied family and friends with a complete itinerary of the *Regina*, so that letters could be sent to various stops along the route. Pam thought with pleasurable anticipation that she might have a letter from Jeff, or from Mother and Ty.

"Sure," Carla agreed, "why not? Of course, somebody may already have picked up the showboat mail, but it won't hurt to see."

They made their way across the street and up the broad stone steps and down an echoing corridor to the General Delivery window. Pam inquired about mail for the Showboat *Regina* and the woman at the window said with a smile, "Oh, yes, it's been accumulating. We wondered when you were due to arrive."

She turned away and returned in a few minutes with a double handful of letters. "You want to take it all?"

"We might as well," Carla said. "Everybody'll be anxious—"

She broke off at the sound of heels clicking rapidly down the hall behind them. She and Pam turned to see Geneva Day hurrying up, her face contorted with anger, her eyes blazing.

"Is that the showboat mail?" she demanded. "Give it to me!" She all but snatched the bundle of letters from the hand of the astonished clerk, then turned her baleful glance on Pam and Carla. "It was my job to pick up the mail today, not yours!"

"Take it easy," Carla said. "What's the difference?"

And Pam added, "We just happened to be across the street and saw the post office, so we thought we'd save someone an extra trip."

Geneva's head was bent as she checked through the mail in her hands. She murmured, "This one's mine, and this and this and this—" Not until she had tucked half a dozen letters into the big pocket of her chintz skirt, did she grudgingly dole out one for Carla and two for Pam. Her aquamarine eyes were still shooting sparks of angry fire as she looked up into Pam's face, ignoring Carla and addressing her rema??s to ?am alone. "I certainly don't see why you had to c??? sneaking in here—"

"Now wait a minute!" Pam ?? ??? in, angry color flooding her face at the other girl ??, ??lting attitude. "We didn't sneak. And what earthly di?. ?nce does it make—"

But Geneva turned on her heel and stalked away, tossing disdainfully over her shoulder, "I'm not going to stand here arguing with you in a public place. You can make an exhibition of yourself if you like!" The sharp click of her high heels receded and was gone.

"Well, I never!" exclaimed the clerk behind the window. "Does she fly off the handle that way very often?"

Pam was so angry she couldn't speak. Tears of humiliation stung at her eyelids.

"What a stinker!" Carla exclaimed with feeling. "Come on, Pam." Together they made their way out into the street. There was no sign of Geneva anywhere.

As they walked along, Carla comforted, "Don't mind her. She's just crazy, blowing up like that! So it was her job to pick up the mail. So what? If Buff knew how she acted about it—"

"But Buff doesn't know." Pam's voice was low and thoughtful. "And he won't know unless we tell him. And we aren't going to tell him, are we, Carla?"

"Well—no," Carla admitted. "I don't suppose we'll stoop to tattling on her. But it makes me mad for her to get away with treating you like that and then being civil enough to you in front of Buff, so that he doesn't realize what's going on."

There was a firm set to Pam's jaw as she answered, "This is between Geneva and me. I don't want Buff bothered with it. He's got enough on his hands without having to cope with a couple of feuding females. I'll handle Geneva myself."

"I suppose that is the best way." Carla shook her head then in rueful reminiscence. "But what a silly scene that was! You'd think we cared how many letters she got, or that we intended to steam them open over a teakettle or something!"

"I don't know what was eating her," Pam agreed. "She got a lot of mail. More than either of us did."

Belatedly, she remembered to look at the two letters Geneva had doled out to her. They were still clutched tight in her fingers. Her heart lifted as she saw that one of them was from Jeff and the other from her mother, with a strange foreign stamp on it. A little grin lifted the corners of Pam's lips as she told Carla, "She ought to know, though, that it's quality that counts and not quantity."

CHAPTER TWELVE

BAD NEWS

As THE SUMMER DAYS slipped past, the showboaters grew to know the river in most of her moods. Calm or stormy, glittering with sunshine or darkly gray and whipped with rain, the Ohio was changeable and fascinating. July brought hot and humid weather, but this didn't deter the showboat audiences in the least. The troupe continued to play to capacity houses, grateful for the little river breeze that usually sprang up with the darkness each evening.

Relationships on the *Regina* became easier and more relaxed as the showboaters got used to each other. The girls no longer cared if they were seen in pin curls during the busy morning hours. And they grew calloused to the recurrent shadow of unshaved beards on masculine chins. A number of romances developed, as Buff could have told them was prac ally inevitable. Whether these would last through the tire season, or fade and die soon after they had reached he pin stage, remained to be seen. Tip Flanders was at lea. temporarily mad over a dark-haired young man named Ca Seaman, who stood six-feet-four in his socks and had a bar one voice that went well with Tip's own rather throaty contralto. They sang a humorous love song in the vaudeville show which usually brought down the house. Quiet little Ellen Carr had exchanged club pins with Rudy Blair and was looking absolutely starry-eyed. And there were several other twosomes that spent most of their time together.

Penny and Mike remained as solid as ever. Pam knew how d p their feeling for each other ran. They would m someday, but they were too sensible to rush into until Mike had finished school and was ready to assume the responsibilities of marriage. His family was not financially capable of helping him through college. He was earning his own way and Penny cared far too much for him to put any stumbling blocks in his path.

How must it feel, Pam sometimes wondered a shade enviously, to be as sure of your love, as confident of the future, as her sister and Mike? She was almost sure she loved Jeff Moore, that she could be happy spending the rest of her life with him. And yet the thought of living on a farm, of adjusting herself to the sort of life Jeff's wife must lead, filled her with dread and uncertainty. But Penny, knowing that Mike wanted to teach and try to write when he had his bachelor's degree, wasn't troubled in the least by the realization that his plans carried with them little promise of much financial reward.

Pam asked Penny once how this could be. She inquired seriously, "Don't you ever get scared and feel unsure about Mike when you think of living in some little house on a school teacher's salary? Not much money for clothes or fun, just struggling to make ends meet?"

Penny laughed a little, shaking her head, her eyes full of dreams. "You make it sound so grim. But it won't be, not with Mike and me together. We won't ever be rich, but we won't care. We'll have so much that's more important than just money. We'll be part of each other and Mike will be doing what he wants to do, work that he feels is important."

Jeff would be doing that on his farm, Pam reminded herself, her gaze thoughtful on Penny's face. He felt, as his father did, that there was no more vital and satisfying work than farming.

Penny went on, "Mike and I were talking about it just the other night. He gets so mad, all this stuff you hear about the disadvantages of teaching. Even if they're not paid as well as they should be, there are so many other values to consider. Mike feels there's nothing more important in the world than helping to shape the minds and abilities of children. They need understanding and guidance more than they may at any other time in their lives." A tender little smile curved Penny's lips as she told Pam, "I came across a quotation one day from Henry Adams. When I told Mike, he said it expressed exactly the way he felt about teaching."

"What was it?"

Penny repeated softly, " 'A teacher affects eternity. He can never tell where his influence stops.' "

Penny would be a good wife for Mike, Pam felt sure. She wished she were as confident that she would be a good wife for Jeff. . . .

Always, running like a dark thread through the clear bright pattern of showboat life, was the continuing enmity between Pam and Geneva Day. Buff seemed unaware of it, which was strange, since he was observant enough in other matters. And he was always stressing the importance of the troupe working together agreeably, helping each other, living in close quarters without getting on each other's nerves.

Once he told them all, during a lazy Sunday afternoon gab session on the upper deck, "The *Regina*'s almost like a desert island. If the lot of us were shipwrecked on her, we'd have to get along together. Not because we're all alike in character or personality, but because we'd have to learn to respect the other fellow's right to be different. That's a good thing for anyone to learn."

Buff's point was logical, Pam admitted. And she didn't care how different Geneva was. But couldn't Buff see that it was Geneva who was always needling her in subtle ways, that the other girl wouldn't let her, Pam, alone? Or was it just that he didn't want to see? Sometimes Pam wondered. Still she tried to put aside the ugly suspicion that Buff might be influenced by the Day family money and the power of Geneva's Uncle Andrew wielded in Harwood College affairs.

Pam had told no one except Penny, who was like another self, about the incident at the post office. And Carla had followed Pam's wish and kept quiet about it, too. So Buff could have no way of knowing about that. But there were other things more obvious, occurrences that had taken place right on the *Regina*. Little things, unimportant in themselves, and yet which added up into an ugly undeniable total. A slighting remark, of the sort Gen was so adept at. The knack of putting Pam in the wrong, so that she appeared to poor advantage. Sometimes it took only a look, or an inflection when she spoke, but the intention to hurt was there, clear and plain to be seen. And yet Buff, whether by accident or intent, failed to observe what was going on. Or at least he did nothing at all about it.

"Maybe he figures," Penny told Pam, "that you'll work things out better between you without any interference on his part. He's had so much experience running the showboat, maybe he's seen feuds like this before and thinks that's the best way to deal with them."

"Maybe," Pam agreed a shade grimly. "But I'm getting pretty sick of her attitude."

"I don't blame you," Penny backed her up staunchly. "I can't figure out why she's so nasty to you—unless it's on account of Alan."

Pam said stubbornly, "I wouldn't give her the satisfaction of letting her have him now, not after the way she's treated me."

"But if he'd break with her completely," Penny frowned as she said, "it would be better. Then she'd know she was out of the running. As it is, he's nice to both of you. Sometimes he concentrates on one and sometimes the other, as if he enjoys keeping you both dangling."

It was Pam's turn to frown. "Dangling? That's a funny way to put it."

Penny shrugged. "I'm sorry, but that's the way it looks from where I sit. He seems to be playing one of you against the other, just trying to make you both jealous and resentful."

"You only think that," Pam accused, "because you don't like him."

"I don't like him nearly as well as Jeff," Penny admitted. "And neither does Mike." She broke off to ask incredulously, "Surely you don't either, Pam?"

Pam said, "No, of course not. But he's fun and available. And Jeff wants me to enjoy my summer, so I mean to. Don't worry, Penny. I'm not falling madly in love. But I'm certainly not going to hand Alan politely over to Geneva. She thinks she's irresistible enough without letting her get the idea she can take Alan away from me. That would really give her something to crow over."

It wasn't long after that conversation when a suspicion began to grow in Pam's mind that she hesitated at first to voice even to Penny. They were playing *Virtue Rewarded* again in a different town and with a changed cast. Now Geneva had the role of Clarabelle, while Pam played the less important character part of the mother.

The calliope concert was in progress and the crowd was already beginning to gather for the evening's performance when Pam, starting to get into costume, discovered that the fastener was missing from the belt of her skirt. She was surprised, since it hadn't seemed loose when she took off the costume the night before. Moreover, not only was the hook missing, but there was no sign of it when she started looking about on the floor above which the costume had hung. Pam had to search hurriedly for another fastener, for a needle and thread to repair the costume. She made her entrance that night slightly out of breath and Geneva smiled a secret little smile that seemed to Pam to have a special significance.

The missing fastener was the first of numerous small mishaps that seemed to overtake Pam with a regularity she, at least, found suspicious. One night her gray wig was missing. It turned up in a corner of the dressing-room behind several voluminous skirts after Pam had hunted for it with increasing anxiety for more than fifteen minutes. Of course, it *could* have fallen there. But Pam rather doubted that it had. Still there was nothing tangible to indicate that Geneva had anything to do with it. Another time it was a parasol, absolutely vital to a part of her stage business, that couldn't be found until a frantic search had ensued. But since props or parts of costume occasionally were mislaid by others than Pam, she couldn't be entirely sure that Geneva was at the root of the misfortunes that seemed to be dogging her.

Pam finally confided to Penny, "Either she is, or I'm just naturally jinxed. I've been having the darnedest time lately. Missing fasteners and disappearing props. Just serious enough to be annoying to me, but nothing so vital that it comes to Buff's attention. She must be behind it all!"

"But you can't be sure," Penny reminded in all fairness. "It could be just accidental. Unless someone catches her in the act, what can you do?"

Pam shrugged. "Exactly what I am doing—nothing! She won't dare try anything serious enough actually to wreck a performance. Then she'd have Buff to cope with and I don't think she'd risk that. But if I'm ever sure she's messing things up for me, she's going to be sorry!"

If Geneva was at the root of Pam's crop of minor misfortunes, she managed to cover her tracks well. Still, Pam suspected her. And the situation between them grew more tense.

Most of the girls around the Hen Roost were on Pam's side. Only a few got on well with Geneva. And these were the ones who catered to her whims, who listened with avid interest to her oft-told stories of the gay life she had left behind temporarily, who were impressed with the quantity of letters she received.

"I try to get my parents not to write me every day," Geneva admitted with an apologetic little smile, "but it's no use."

There was no question but that she got more mail than anyone else aboard the *Regina*. She had persuaded Mary to give her the regular job of going to the post office each day. It didn't matter to any of the others, but Geneva acted as though her mail was so important she couldn't wait to get it. And she always went off by herself to answer her letters, instead of scribbling casually away in the Hen Roost as all the others did.

As if, Pam sometimes thought resentfully, she's afraid some of us might try to peek over her shoulder!

It certainly didn't matter to Pam how many letters Geneva got. The twins heard from their parents almost every week. And Jeff wrote Pam more often than that. He might not be a very fluent correspondent, but the sight of his big scrawling writing on an envelope gave her a tremendous lift just the same.

One of Jeff's letters told her that his father had had a serious heart attack and was having to spend most of his time in bed. "It's all Mom and I can do to keep him there," Jeff wrote, "since he's feeling a little better. But we're going to follow the doctor's orders if we have to sit on Dad to hold him down. But, as you can see, this doesn't give me any chance to visit you, much as I want to. So just remember I love you and I'm missing you a lot and hope you're doing the same. It's possible my sister and her husband may come here to live later on. With George to take over some of the work, I wouldn't be so tied down. As things are, I won't even be able to go back to school this fall, unless Fannie and George do come. So keep your fingers crossed for me."

For us, Pam's heart amended as she read the letter. It would be awful not to have Jeff at school, not to be able to see him all the time as she'd counted on doing. But that was a rather selfish attitude, she realized. She felt sincerely sorry for Jeff, sensing between the lines of his letter his anxiety for his father, his uncertainty over all his future plans. Jeff wanted so much to finish college. And his father also wanted him to do so. Pam remembered them all so clearly. She had spent Thanksgiving at the Moore farm last fall, had met Jeff's married sister and her pleasant young husband, who lived in a small city not very far away. And Pam had liked them, just as she liked Jeff's white-haired energetic mother, his lively younger brother and sister. It was a sad thing to think of the shadow of Mr. Moore's serious illness hanging over them all, dampening the fun and companionship Pam knew bound the whole family so closely together.

The news in Jeff's letter made her own trouble with Geneva seem trivial and unimportant. Pam knew how she'd feel if her mother were dangerously ill. No doubt Jeff was just as worried about his father.

When she wrote, she would tell him how sorry she was, and that she would be hoping and praying for his father's recovery. And she would assure him of her love, so that he wouldn't have that to worry about in addition to everything else. She would tell him, too, that she understood why he couldn't come to see her, that she didn't blame him in the least.

If only, Pam thought, she could be there with Jeff to express her thoughts in person. Trying to put words down on paper, serious, sympathetic words, was so hard. The pressure of her arms about him, her lips touching his, could make her love and understanding so much plainer to him. But since they couldn't be together, she would do the best she could by means of a letter.

Poor Jeff. . . .

CHAPTER THIRTEEN

VISITORS FROM HOME

LATE IN JULY the twins' mother wrote that she and Ty were planning to drive out to visit them the following week end. They had only been back from their honeymoon a few weeks. "But," Celia's letter said, "we are both so anxious to see you and that fabulous showboat. Our respective businesses seemed to get on all right without us while we were away, so we decided we could take a few more days off and pay you a short visit."

Pam and Penny were delighted at the prospect of seeing Mother and Ty, of having the other showboaters meet them. The day of their arrival coincided with the opening of a new play, one in which both the twins had fairly important parts. So their excitement and anticipation mounted as the day wore on and the hour of their parents' expected coming drew near.

It was late afternoon when Celia and Ty ascended the *Regina*'s gangplank. The twins, who had been looking for them ever since their own return from the showboat parade, fell upon them with delighted cries of greeting and queries as to what had delayed them.

"We stopped at the hotel to freshen up," Celia explained. "It's been a long drive and we didn't want to disgrace you."

Their mother seemed younger and lovelier than ever before. A smart white suit showed off her tropical tan in spectacular fashion. Ty, tall and spare, looked distinguished in gray slacks and a jaunty checked sport jacket. And both of them were beaming. One look was all it took for Pam and Penny to realize that they were more in love than ever.

As the four of them stood there, chattering happily, asking questions and answering them in the same breath with more questions, Pam felt the warmth of being with Mother and Ty again welling up in her. Penny, too, must be experiencing the same wonderful awareness that they were a family now, complete with the customary number of parents. Celia had tried so hard to keep the death of their own father years before from shadowing their lives. Still, despite her efforts, there had been an emptiness, a lack. And now Ty was filling it. Pam knew the others were sharing this happy knowledge, although no word was spoken. Some things went too deep for a need of words.

After those first moments, there were introductions to be made. Proudly the twins took Mother and Ty around, showing them the *Regina*, presenting the other members of the troupe to them.

Mike exclaimed, "Gee, it's swell to see you, Mrs. Howard—I mean—" he gulped in embarrassment, "M-mrs. Shelton."

Celia, greeting him warmly, laughed a little at his discomfiture. "Never mind, Mike. You're not the first person to stumble over my new name."

And Ty chuckled, as he and Mike shook hands. "It just takes practice. And you'll have plenty of time for that, because she's going to be Mrs. Shelton for a long, long while."

Buff, with Aunt Lucy's approval, invited the Sheltons to have dinner aboard the *Regina*. And they accepted with pleasure. Now there would be no need for them to go back to their hotel before the night's performance, which meant that they'd have just that much more time to spend with the twins on the showboat.

Pam and Penny took their mother to the Hen Roost to get cleaned up for dinner. The big untidy room was crowded with girls, talking and powdering their noses and applying lipstick. Just inside the door the twins came face to face with Geneva Day. She hadn't been around when Celia met all the others, whether intentionally or not, Pam wasn't sure. And, of course, Celia knew nothing of the bad feeling between them.

Now Geneva stood there, her faint smile inscrutable, as Penny's introduction sounded loud in the sudden silence. Her politely murmured, "How do you do," was completely impersonal.

"Hello, Geneva." Celia held out her hand in her usual friendly fashion and Geneva took it rather slowly. But Celia was quite unaware of any hesitancy on her part. "It's so nice," she smiled, "to have a chance to meet all Pam's and Penny's friends."

A little, but only a little, more warmth filtered into Geneva's smile. Or was she simply being amused, Pam wondered, by Celia's unknowing assumption that they were friends?

Celia talked on pleasantly for a moment or two. And Geneva responded, not quite so stiffly on guard as she had been at first. But this was no particular concession on Geneva's part, Pam thought, since it would have taken a stone statue to resist the sincere friendliness of Mother's manner. Too bad she was wasting her time being nice to Geneva, who certainly didn't care, one way or the other.

Dinner was even gayer than usual, its lively talkative atmosphere enhanced by Celia's and Ty's presence, as well as by the exciting imminence of another opening night. The Sheltons entered so happily into the spirit of it all that one would have thought they were going to take part in the performance, too. Pam could see that Buff and the other members of the staff were as drawn to them as she had expected they'd be. And a quiet pride filled her over her parents' popularity.

Celia and Ty lingered on deck to hear and see the calliope concert, while the twins went off to the dressing room backstage to get into costume. When Celia stuck her head around the edge of the door almost half an hour later, to wish all the girls luck, she saw Pam, with Penny's help, working hard to sew a loose-trailing flounce back onto the full skirt of Pam's costume. The crowded little room was hot and stuffy and Pam looked almost ready to cry with vexation.

"Dear, what happened?" Celia exclaimed. "Did you step on it?"

"No," Pam's voice was flat, as her mother took the needle from her none-too-steady fingers and proceeded to help repair the damage with quick skillful stitches.

"Then how on earth—?" Celia asked.

Pam said tautly, "It was that way when I went to put the costume on. Yesterday at dress rehearsal, it was okay. But things like that are always happening to me lately. It's very strange."

Across the room Geneva was putting the finishing touch to her make-up at the big mirror. She made no move to indicate she'd heard what Pam was saying. Her expression, reflected in the glass, remained blandly detached, as though Pam's misfortunes had nothing at all to do with her. But there was sharp tension in the room among the other girls. Celia, busy with her needle, was the only one who remained unaware of it.

In a few moments the costume was repaired. Penny moved off, a faint frown between her eyes, to tie on her bonnet and take a last look at herself in the mirror. Pam slipped into her costume with a murmured word of thanks and her mother zipped her up and fluffed out her skirt ruffles.

"There, dear," Celia said, giving her shoulder a little affectionate pat, "you look lovely. You all do," she added, smiling at the other girls. And she cried, as she turned toward the doorway, "Good luck, everybody."

It seemed to Pam, whose eyes were fixed on Geneva, that the other girl's glance followed Celia from the room in a rather oddly intent manner.

The performance went off well for a first night and the audience responded with even more than its customary uninhibited enthusiasm. During one tense scene, in which the hero was searching everywhere for the villain, Alan hammed things up by walking so closely behind him they were practically in lockstep. Finally one

92

feminine observer could stand it no longer. She cried out, "He's right there! Right behind you!" In the ripple of startled amusement that followed her outcry, Alan stepped to the front of the stage and informed her confidentially, "Look, lady. We've been rehearsing this for a week. He knows I'm right behind him!" Then in the deafening roar of laughter that burst not only from the audience but from the cast as well, he went calmly back to his dogging of the hero's footsteps once more and the play continued.

Afterward, at the buffet supper in the dining cabin, Celia exclaimed, "I have never laughed so hard in my life! That play was the funniest thing I ever saw. I think you're all perfectly wonderful."

"So do I," Ty agreed. He told Buff, "If you put on shows like this in the cities, I should think you could make a fortune."

Buff chuckled. "Maybe. But city audiences might brush us off as too corny." He helped himself to another sugared doughnut from the big plateful Aunt Lucy had made especially for the occasion. "We did play six solid weeks in Pittsburgh one year, though, with capacity houses, too. Only reason we had to pull anchor then was because we were all due back at college. But the fact is," he admitted, "I'd rather play smaller towns. I think it's a more rounded experience for the troupe to move from place to place, perform for different types of audiences, rather than stay tied up half the summer near some big city."

"I suppose it is," Ty agreed. "I keep forgetting this isn't primarily a commercial venture."

"That's it," Buff nodded. "It's a college course and we mean to keep it operating in such a way that it does the most for the students. We only have to be commercial enough," he added drily, "to stay out of the red. And so far we've done that."

Pam was more quiet than usual during supper. The memory of that ripped flounce on her costume kept coming back to her. Had Geneva slipped into the dressing room unobserved and done it deliberately? Pam felt almost sure of it, yet her dislike of Geneva might be warping her judgment. And how was she ever going to know?

Her annoyance was further augmented by the fact that Alan was being unusually attentive to Geneva. That, Pam reminded herself grimly, she couldn't be imagining. After weeks of devoting the greater part of his time to Pam, he seemed to have done a complete about-face. Why, she couldn't imagine. They hadn't quarreled, there'd been no difficulty between them. And yet Alan was treating her as though she were no more important to him than any other casual acquaintance. Was it because her parents were there and he didn't want to intrude? Or had Geneva's untiring efforts to win him back succeeded finally?

Pam came up out of the depths of her brooding abstraction to hear Mother and Ty inviting all the showboaters to have dinner with them at their hotel the following day. "You've been so very hospitable to us," Ty said, "we'd like a chance to entertain you."

And Mother added, smiling, "Since it's Sunday, you won't have to put on a show. So do come, all of you."

In the pleased murmur of agreement all about, not one dissenting voice was raised. Buff thanked the Sheltons and accepted for everyone. Pam felt her smile grow fixed and hot anger rise within her, all the more scorching because it had to be concealed. How could Geneva have the effrontery to come, after the way she'd acted? Pam looked across the room to where the other girl stood, close beside Alan, smiling up into his attentive face. It wouldn't be easy for Pam to treat her graciously tomorrow. And yet, unless she wanted her mother and Ty to realize the full extent of their enmity, she'd have to cloak her true feelings in surface politeness.

The Sheltons' big dinner party filled half the hotel dining room. Celia and Ty were so cordially agreeable and the showboaters in such holiday spirits that everyone had a wonderful time. Even Pam, by keeping as far as possible away from Geneva, managed to enjoy herself.

Aunt Lucy said feelingly, "It's such a treat to eat a meal you haven't planned for a change."

"Or one you didn't peel the spuds for," someone amended.

And everyone laughed.

They lingered long over dessert and coffee. No one wanted to make the first move toward breaking up such a good party. But at last it was time to go and there was a flurry of thanks and farewells, since the Sheltons would be leaving early the next day.

Pam and Penny stayed on for a while after the others left. They accompanied Mother and Ty up to their comfortable suite for a final private talk.

Mother, settling herself on the couch between the twins, asked, "You're both enjoying the showboat, aren't you?"

"Oh, yes," Penny and Pam answered in one breath. And Pam added, "It's a wonderful experience, one we'll never forget."

"Such a nice crowd of young people!" Mother exclaimed.

"Yes, most of them are," Pam added.

Ty remarked, lighting his pipe, "I suppose there's sure to be some friction among that many kids living in such close quarters. But I expect Buff sees to it that no serious trouble develops. He seems pretty capable of keeping things under control."

Pam flashed Penny an unobtrusive warning look. She didn't want her parents dragged in on the situation between her and Geneva, any more than she cared to have it called to Buff's attention.

But all Penny said was, "Oh, of course, there are some we're more congenial with than others. But that's only natural." The faint smile she gave Pam was reassuring.

"Do you know," Mother said thoughtfully, kicking off her high-heeled slippers and tucking her feet under her as she loved to do, "who interested me most?"

"Alan?" Pam guessed. "He's so attractive."

"He is that," Celia nodded. "And a good actor, too."

"And knows it," Ty added drily.

"Don't be catty, dear." Celia reached over to pat his hand. "Men aren't supposed to be, you know. Actually," she went on, her tone thoughtful, "the one I find intriguing is Geneva."

Pam frowned in surprise. "But why?"

And Penny said, "She's one of the hardest of all to get along with."

Mother nodded. "I expect she is. People with inferiority complexes aren't usually easy to live with, or to understand."

"Inferiority?" Pam tried to keep her tone casual. "I should say it's more of a superiority complex that's bothering her."

"The symptoms," Ty mused, "are often interchangeable. It's only human to try to mask feelings of inferiority by pretending to think you're better than anyone else."

"But what's she got to feel inferior about?" Pam managed a light laugh. "Practically all the money in the world, doting parents, more friends than she needs—and on top of it all, she's beautiful."

"Yes," Mother agreed, "that's what makes her so interesting. I can't figure her out. But she's not a person I'll forget."

She's one I wish I could, Pam thought tartly. But of course she kept her opinion to herself.

CHAPTER FOURTEEN

BUFF TAKES A HAND

The morning after Celia's and Ty's brief visit, Penny happened to be on K P with Geneva. As Penny washed and the other girl dried the stacks of dishes and silver that were the aftermath of every showboat meal, Geneva unbent sufficiently to say, "Your parents are nice. I like them."

"Thanks." Penny's smile was friendly. "I'm pretty fond of them myself."

But Geneva's lovely face remained grave. She dried a cup with more than customary thoroughness before continuing thoughtfully, "They haven't been married very long, have they?"

Penny shook her head. "Just since June."

"Divorced?" Geneva pressed. "Your real father, I mean."

"No," Penny told her, a little catch in her voice, "he was killed in an auto accident years ago."

"Oh, I'm sorry," Geneva said politely, but with no real regret in her voice. She set the cup down on the cabinet and picked up another. "If anything like that happened to my father, it would just kill my mother, too. They're so close."

Penny tried to keep the annoyance she felt from sounding in her tone. Maybe Geneva didn't realize how rude her remark was. Penny told her, "You can't just stop living when someone you love dies. Mother had us to take care of, she had to work hard to support us. She couldn't give in to grief and feeling sorry for herself."

"No, I suppose not," Geneva said, having the grace to sound a little apologetic. She added, "Your stepfather's nice, too, almost as nice as your mother. They're both so—" she groped for the right word, "so warm and kind, as if they like everyone. My parents are that way, too," she told Penny. "Maybe that's why I liked yours so, because they reminded me of mine—oh, not in looks, of course, but in their ways. And they're so much in love —anyone can see that, and so very fond of you and your sister." She was silent a moment, then added almost defensively, "My parents would come to visit me, if it weren't so terribly far for them."

"Of course." Penny nodded.

Afterward, telling Pam about that rather curious conversation, Penny admitted, "For some crazy reason I felt sort of sorry for her. Oh, I know she's been awful to you, but—I can't seem to forget that idea of Mother's that she might have an inferiority complex. Do you suppose she could?"

"Why on earth should she?" Pam dismissed the notion.

"I can't imagine," Penny said. "She's got everything and yet—well, sometimes it's as if she's trying to prove how terrific she and her family and their possessions are. And would she do that," Penny wondered aloud, "if she really had any sense of security?"

"I don't know," Pam said bluntly, "and I don't care." She certainly had more important things to do than to waste time pondering the quirks of Geneva's strange personality.

Not long after that Buff Quinn made an opportunity to talk privately with Pam. He called her into the deserted ticket office on the pretext of discussing one of the scenes in the current play. But this minor matter was settled in a few minutes. Then Buff got around to his real reason for wanting to talk with her.

"I understand," he said, hooking his heels through the rungs of his chair and leaning his elbows on his knees to look quizzically into Pam's face, "that you've been having some trouble lately."

"Trouble?" Pam frowned, wondering exactly what he was getting at and not wanting to commit herself until she was sure.

Buff nodded and brushed one hand back and forth across the stubble of his brown hair. "Nothing big and important," he grinned. "I hope you'd come to me about anything vital. Just little stuff, but bothersome. A kind of jinx, you might call it."

Pam smiled back at him a trifle uncertainly. She wondered who had told Buff, and how much he knew. Annoyance flooded over her at the unknown outsider's interference. She thought everyone had understood she didn't want Buff brought in on her private feud with Geneva. But there was no use dwelling on that now. Aloud she said, "Well, yes, I have been sort of prone to accidents lately."

"Like ripping the flounce on your costume the other night without knowing how it happened," Buff enumerated in his quiet easy way. "And losing things."

His glance was so steady that Pam's eyes fell before its probing penetration. She nodded, rubbing at a mud splash on her jeans as though it were very important to remove it. After a moment's stretching silence, she murmured, "I wish you hadn't been bothered about it. I didn't want anyone to tell you."

"No one did," Buff replied quietly. "No one person, that is. But you kids must think I'm blind not to see things that go on right under my nose. The showboat's too small a world for aloof detachment. Everything is everybody's business and things have to keep on an even keel or we're all in trouble. I could quote Donne," he said, his eyes crinkling a little with a smile that didn't quite reach his lips, "and say, 'No man is an island.' But that's getting a bit hackneyed, so I won't. What I really want, Pam," he went on succinctly, "is your candid opinion. If you feel Geneva's to blame for your jinx, I want you to say so." He added then, "I've known all along there was friction between you, but I thought it would blow over."

"I thought so, too," Pam admitted. "I'm still hoping, but it doesn't seem very likely. I can't understand her."

"You haven't answered my question," Buff prodded.

Pam said slowly, wanting to be fair, "I'm not sure Geneva's had any part in the crazy things that have been happening to me. I have a feeling, but feelings don't prove anything. Maybe it's just her attitude and the fact that we're not very congenial that makes me suspect her."

There was a gleam of admiration in Buff's clear glance. "I'm glad you're not convinced she's to blame, with nothing tangible to go on. Sometimes a lot of queer things happen that are nobody's doing. I'd hate to crack down on anyone undeservedly. But if you have any shred of actual proof that she's at the root of your troubles, I want you to let me know."

Pam shook her head in the negative. She had no proof. But she wasn't sure she'd tell Buff about it if she had. She still felt she'd rather handle the situation herself.

Buff went on, his tone thoughtful, "Confidentially, I've wondered some whether I made a mistake in accepting her for the course. The way she was so late getting here and all she put us through then. And her personality isn't the sort that makes for easy adjustment. But there were circumstances . . ." He didn't go into them, however. Instead, he said, "Anyway, she's here and I hope things work out."

Pam said, "I've tried to get along with her. I'll keep on trying. But I simply won't let her push me around."

"No one expects that," Buff told her. He rose and Pam got to her feet, too, realizing that their discussion was over. "I wonder," the professor rubbed at his close-cropped head again as they moved toward the door, "whether it might be better if you two talked things over, instead of keeping your feelings all bottled up inside of you."

Pam's tone was dry, answering, "We just don't have much to say to each other, I'm afraid. . . ."

When, only a few days later, Pam discovered that she and Geneva had been assigned to do the marketing together, she couldn't help suspecting that Buff had done some manipulating. The daily work schedule was still Mary Hatcher's responsibility. But Mary, knowing how strained relations were between Pam and Geneva, would scarcely have thrown them together except at Buff's suggestion. He might just figure this enforced proximity would give them a chance to straighten out their difficulties. Had he also, Pam wondered, had a session with Gen besides the one with her?

As they walked down the gangplank, Geneva a few steps in the lead, Pam could almost feel the sparks of animosity emanating from the other girl. She debated whimsically with herself whether to reach out and touch Gen and see if she got a shock. The idea made her smile a little and she was still smiling as she and Geneva reached the station wagon.

"You want to drive," Pam asked, "or shall I?"

"I will," Geneva said flatly, sliding in under the wheel. Pam had no choice but to climb in beside her.

It was a two-mile drive to the highway super market and vegetable stand which was their destination. Geneva was a smoothly competent driver. Probably, Pam thought, she was one of those lucky creatures who had been given a convertible for her sixteenth birthday and had been driving ever since. The morning was sunny and clear and Pam leaned back comfortably to enjoy the drive in the fresh sweet air. Geneva had spoken no word since they climbed into the station wagon and the grim set of her jaw led Pam to think she had no intention of talking.

So, I can be stubborn, too, Pam thought, turning her head a little to let her glance roam appreciatively over the passing landscape.

Suddenly, Geneva braked so unexpectedly that Pam jerked forward and put out a hand to brace herself from bumping the windshield. A rabbit scurried into the greenery that edged the road. "Sorry," Geneva said, as the car picked up speed once more. "I didn't want to hit it."

Pam didn't blame her. She always felt a little sick when a car she was riding in hit anything even as small as a swooping sparrow. Now Geneva's matching squeamishness seemed to make for a slight bond between them and Pam felt a shade more friendly toward her.

On an abrupt impulse, she said, "Gen I think we should get some things cleared up between us."

"Why?" The other girl's profile looked cool and withdrawn as her lips emitted the single syllable. She continued to give her full attention to the road ahead.

"Because it's crazy to go on this way," Pam said quietly. "Sitting here a few inches apart and not speaking—does that make sense?"

Geneva's only answer was a slight shrug, contemptuous in its implications. Her shrug said plainly that she preferred to let the matter drop. But Pam, now that she had begun talking, found herself bent on following Buff's advice, on bringing out into the open all the old hurts and resentments that had rankled between them so long. Maybe a good airing would help, just as Buff had said.

She told Geneva, "You've had it in for me all summer. First because Buff gave me a part you thought you were entitled to and then—" she hesitated, but only momentarily, "because of Alan."

Geneva slowed the station wagon, then steered it off

101

the road and braked to a halt on the wide shoulder. She turned toward Pam, her eyes blazing. "Buff never would have given you my part if you hadn't worked on him behind my back, convinced him I wasn't going to get here in time."

Pam could only exclaim in astonishment, "I didn't—"

Then Geneva was rushing on, still in that biting angry voice, "As for Alan Richmond, surely even someone as stupid as you can see he's not important to me. He's just someone for kicks on this pokey old showboat cruise. I wouldn't bother with him at all, if you weren't so anxious to get him."

As hot words of denial rose to Pam's lips, she found herself remembering that heartbroken sound of weeping she had overheard the night of Geneva's quarrel with Alan. It had been Geneva, somehow she felt sure of it now. And despite Geneva's attempt to disguise the fact, Pam realized that Alan really meant a lot to her and that she was sick with fear at the possibility of losing him.

Unwilling pity stirred in Pam, cooling her anger. She was surprised at the calmness of her tone as she told Geneva, "I'm certainly not in love with Alan, either. We're just friends."

"If it weren't to hurt you," Geneva said slowly, "I wouldn't even want him for a friend. Nor you, either! Is that quite clear?"

Pam felt quick color flame in her face. Still, she managed to hang on to her temper. She said as slowly, as distinctly as Geneva had spoken, "We needn't be friends if you don't want to. It doesn't matter to me. But if you keep on trying to make trouble for me, Buff won't put up with it."

A trace of uneasiness clouded the other girl's eyes. All Geneva said, though, was, "Who's making trouble?"

"Someone seems to be," Pam told her. "And Buff has asked me to let him know if I'm sure it's you."

"But you're not sure, are you?" Geneva's tone was disdainful.

"Not yet," Pam admitted. "But I've got a pretty strong hunch. And one of these times I'll find out for sure." She paused a second, then decided to make one more effort. "Even so," she said quietly, "I'd rather we could work things out ourselves. I don't want to get you into a jam."

"How sweet!" Geneva drawled. "I should think you'd like nothing better."

She swung the car back onto the road once more and Pam made no effort to talk further. It would only be a waste of time she felt.

CHAPTER FIFTEEN

TROUBLE FOR JEFF

THE SERIES OF minor mishaps that had haunted Pam stopped abruptly after her talk with Geneva. Actually, Pam felt, you couldn't ask for stronger proof that Gen had been at the root of them. But she had no intention of pointing this out to Buff. Pam was quite willing to let the matter rest. As she admitted to Penny, "I'm just thankful she's scared enough of Buff so that she figures she'd better stop riding me."

"So am I," Penny agreed.

They had been memorizing lines together for the play now in rehearsal. Both of them knew it wa￼ ￼me to go down and get ready for dinner, still they leaned for a few quiet moments longer on the upper deck rail. It was shady and cool here and they were enjoying their chance for private conversation.

Penny went on, "I'm glad you had that talk with her, though. Now she knows you're willing to meet her halfway."

"Halfway?" Pam's smile was rueful. "Seems to me I've gone a good two-thirds. But Geneva wants no part of me. She made that painfully clear."

"She hasn't been quite so aloof with me lately," Penny admitted. "But I still can't figure her out. It's as though she's afraid to have anyone get too close to her, to be very friendly. Why would a person feel like that, I wonder?"

Pam didn't know. "She's like that with everybody," she pointed out, "not just you. Even the kids who butter her up and hang after her—she holds them off, too."

Penny thought about it for a minute. Then she said, "It's as if she draws a line beyond which she doesn't want anyone to go. As if—she doesn't trust people, or as if there's something she doesn't want them to know. Such a strange girl. I wish I could figure her out."

"Well, you haven't got time to do it before dinner," Pam said. She linked her arm through Penny's. "Come on, we have to get washed up."

"Okay." Penny smiled. "But Geneva's interesting to think about. And—who knows?—maybe sometime I'll discover the key to why she acts the way she does."

For some reason that final, only half-serious remark of Penny's lingered in Pam's mind. What was the key to Geneva, she wondered? Or did she have one? Or was she simply locked within herself, with no chance to escape from the unguessed twists and turnings of her strange personality?

And now Alan Richmond did one of his inexplicable about-faces and began paying more attention to Pam. As usual there seemed to be no reason for his change of heart. Certainly Pam hadn't gone out of her way to win him over. And if he and Geneva had quarreled again, there was no news of it along the showboat grapevine. Yet his renewed interest in Pam showed itself in numerous undeniable ways. He concentrated on her at mealtime. He sought her out during his leisure moments. And whenever the *Regina* tied up at a new town, he asked her to go exploring.

It was on one of these jaunts that they happened to pass a pawnshop where a secondhand guitar was displayed for sale in a dingy window. Alan stopped stock still at sight of it.

"Just what I want!" he exclaimed, his dark eyes glinting with acquisitive enthusiasm. "Come on, Pam. I'm going in and buy it if it's in decent shape."

"Crazy!" Pam objected. "What do you want with that?"

"What our vaudeville show needs," Alan informed her, "is a good folk singer. Can't you just hear me strumming my guitar and singing 'Foggy, Foggy Dew' and all forty odd verses of 'Barb'ry Allen'?"

Pam had to laugh, going with him into the musty little shop. Fickle he undoubtedly was and far too sure of his own attractiveness, but he was never dull. All a girl had to do was remember not to take him too seriously. Then she'd be all right.

Pam knew she was in no danger of getting emotionally involved with Alan. But she wasn't so sure Geneva had been telling the truth about her feelings.

Alan carried the old guitar lovingly along all the rest of that evening. It occupied the extra chair at their table when they ate dinner. And afterward, since there was no movie around they cared to see, they wandered into the town's pleasant little park. Here they sat for a while on a bench and Alan picked out chords and hummed softly under his breath. But there was no one about except themselves, so presently he began putting words to the haunting old tune.

" 'When I was a young man, I lived by myself,' " he sang, keeping his excellent baritone low and soft, " 'and worked at the weaver's trade.' "

When he had sung the song through to the last "foggy, foggy dew," Pam found her throat thick and her eyes misty.

"That was beautiful," she told him simply. "I never knew you could sing like that, so moving and intimate."

Alan grinned and laid his hand on hers. "You liked?"

Pam nodded. "Anybody would. Buff will put it in the show for sure."

Alan said, his voice more serious than usual, "Well, we'll see. I hope so, because it's something different, an angle of show business I haven't tried before. And I want to learn them all." He went on, "Maybe I'm nuts. I haven't any idea if I'll ever be good enough to get anywhere. All I know is I've got to try." He asked then,

"You're not figuring seriously on the stage, are you, Pam?"

She shook her head. She loved college dramatics and the showboat, but the professional theater seemed like a wholly improbable dream to her.

Alan continued, "I didn't think so. None of the kids feel about it as I do. Oh, maybe a couple of them think they might teach speech or something. But—it's like a fever in me, Pam. Audiences and lights, all the rush and excitement of it. I'll probably end up a broken-down hack playing bit parts but—"

"No, you won't," Pam said sincerely. "You've got something, Alan. And if you really try, I think you'll make it."

His teeth flashed white in the moonlight as he grinned. "The little woman, urging me on, having confidence in me—that's the stuff, baby. I need it."

He put his arm around her, but Pam drew away from him.

"Don't, Alan." She spoke softly.

"Why not?" he asked in surprise.

"Because neither of us means it," Pam told him. "Just for kicks—" she broke off, a little surprised to hear herself quoting Geneva, then continued, "that's all your relationship with any girl amounts to, isn't it?"

"Well, yes," Alan admitted. "Now that you put it to me so flatly, I guess it's true. But—"

"I don't care," Pam told him, smiling a little. She thought of Jeff and felt the warm reality of her feeling for him rush around her heart. Alan wasn't important enough to her to make any difference between her and Jeff. They were friends in a casual amusing way—that was all they'd ever be. But she was almost sure Geneva's feelings were more deeply involved with Alan, despite her pretense to the contrary. Before she could stop the words, Pam heard herself asking, "But what about Gen?"

Silence hung between them for a moment. Probably, Pam thought, he was wondering what earthly business of hers it was. She rather wondered herself. And yet, somehow, she wasn't sorry she had asked the question.

"Well, yes," Alan said presently. "There's Gen. She's —sort of a problem."

"Why?" Pam asked.

Alan said slowly, "I started dating her at school last year because she's a beautiful dish and I have a normal male weakness for beautiful dishes. That," he added, "was also what drew me to you."

"Never mind the flattery." Pam smiled faintly. "Go on."

"It didn't take long," Alan admitted, "for me to learn that there's a possessive streak in Gen a mile wide. She began to consider me her personal property, hung with Hands Off signs and chained to her for all time. That," Alan said simply, "I couldn't have. With my plans for the future, I'm not ready to settle down with anybody, no matter how gorgeous she is, nor how filthy rich, although that's quite an asset."

"So?"

He fingered a couple of plaintive chords from the guitar on his lap before he answered. "So I figured this summer would be a good time to let Gen know the score. I found myself liking another girl quite a lot, spending a good deal of time with her, so Gen should have got the idea. But Gen—" he hesitated a moment, "well, she clings. And I hate to hurt her. She kind of worries me. I'm not sure how she'd take it if I came out flatly and told her we're through. She's really a strange kid."

"Yes, I know." Pam nodded. Pity for Geneva stirred in her heart. Pretending to Pam to be so casual about Alan, and yet unwilling to let him go, even when she must sense he wanted to. One would think her pride would stop her.

Alan went on, almost as if he were talking to himself, "I can't understand her. She's got looks and money, parents who dote on her, plenty of friends. But I've never known anyone with such a basic sense of insecurity as she has. Now you—" he smiled at Pam, "I can tell you straight out that my intentions aren't serious. And you don't care. But Gen—" he shook his head and sighed.

107

Pam thought, That's because I'm not in love with you and Gen may well be. The difference is, I've got someone else whose intentions are serious, who's only waiting for me to make up my mind.

It struck her in that moment that her mind was made up, that she had grown sure about Jeff without knowing exactly when it had happened. She knew beyond all shadow of doubt that she loved him, that she wanted to marry him later on. At the realization happiness swelled in her, warmly, richly, and she drew a deep, shaken breath.

"But," Alan said firmly, "let's not spoil this evening worrying about Gen. I had no intention of crying on your shoulder, believe me." He plucked a chord, inquiring, "Shall we sing?"

"Why not?" Pam laughed. She had never felt more like singing in her life.

" 'Barb'ry Allen'?" he suggested.

But Pam shook her head. "I know only half the verses. Let's sing 'Blue-tailed Fly.' It's more cheerful."

"Okay." Allen started to tap his foot. "Let's go."

So they sang the lively old song through, their voices clear and true in the little deserted park. And summer moonlight filtered down through the trees and made a lacy pattern all about them. By the time they had finished, the problem of Geneva had faded into the background of Pam's consciousness. Also, by that time, a small, but enthusiastic crowd of listeners had congregated. Pam and Alan were startled by a spattering of applause and a feminine voice asking, "Do you know 'Lonesome Road'?"

"Sure," Alan said agreeably.

So he and Pam sang the haunting spiritual and half a dozen other songs before Alan got to his feet finally and said, "That's all for now, folks. If you want to hear more, come to the showboat. We open tomorrow."

There was laughter, and good-humored calls of "We'll do that" and "Thanks for the performance" were heard all about.

Pam told Alan, as they left the park and started back

108

toward the dock, "I'll bet we drummed up some business without even trying."

"Sure, we did," Alan agreed. "We'll have to get Buff to put that duet of ours into the show. We're not half bad."

Pam laughed. "Those people must think we're a pair of screwballs, singing on a park bench like that."

"Who cares?" Alan shrugged. "It'll just verify their idea that all stage people are nuts."

They strolled back down the steeply descending street that led to the river. Ahead, the *Regina* loomed, her banners fluttering ghostly pale in the gentle breeze, her riding lights glowing in the dark.

As Pam preceded Alan up the gangplank she heard a soft whisper of footsteps approaching along the deck. It was Penny, in robe and slippers, moving toward them through the shadows.

"Pam," Penny's voice sounded anxious, "this wire came for you a little while ago."

She extended her hand toward Pam with the envelope in it. Pam felt a finger of fear touch her heart. But it couldn't be bad news from home, or it would have come to both her and Penny. What could it be then?

She slid her finger under the flap of the envelope, tearing the paper. Alan flicked on his cigarette lighter and held the flame up so that she could see to read the single line of printing glued to the yellow page. Her eyes went first to the signature, "Jeff," then frowning she studied the words above.

"My father died this afternoon," read the wire. "Funeral Wednesday. Can you come?"

CHAPTER SIXTEEN

A SAD TRIP

PAM SAT WITH the Moore family in the little white church, with its reaching spire and stained-glass windows, listening to the words of the minister. The service was a simple one, moving and sincere, as this kindly old man spoke of Charles Moore, who had been his good friend and was now dead.

The country church was filled with friends and neighbors and the scent of flowers lay sweet and heavy on the warm air. Pam sat beside Jeff and felt in some small measure the loss that was so devastating to all of them. If there were only something real and tangible that she could do, she thought, her throat thick with unshed tears. But what comfort could an outsider offer? And she was an outsider, to everyone but Jeff. Not that his mother or the rest of the family hadn't seemed grateful for her coming. Even in their grief they had tried to make her welcome. But there was so little she could do to help.

As was the country custom, close friends had taken over the work of the household, had prepared and brought to the Moore farm every variety of delicious food. In this way they sought to express the reality of their sympathy. There hadn't been any work left for Pam to do. And Jeff's mother clung to him so, Pam and he had scarcely had a chance for a word together. Not that Pam blamed Mrs. Moore. She could undersand her grief so well. Jeff was her older son, a bulwark of strength in this sad time. Naturally he was the one she turned to for help in every decision.

And yet Pam wondered, fleetingly, whether all the changes and adjustments that had taken place on the *Regina* in order for her to be gone this whole day, had been really worth while. But that wasn't the right way to look at it, she knew. Jeff had wanted her, had needed her. And she had been just as anxious to be with him, to give him, if only by her presence, all the comfort she could. But was that enough, she asked herself? A feeling of inadequacy and failure lay like a shadow across her spirit.

When the funeral was over, Pam went home with the Moores from the little hillside cemetery. Late afternoon sunshine streamed as brightly into the big pleasant farmhouse as though death hadn't entered there. And yet Pam was aware of the emptiness and loss that weighed so heavily on all of them. But because her grief was so much less than theirs, she felt like an intruder. After all, she had only met Jeff's father a few times. He was an integral part of the lives of all the others.

As though sensing Pam's feelings, Jeff's mother came up to her and took her hands gently. Sunshine touched her white hair and ravaged face, and her eyes, hazel as Jeff's were, seemed kind. She said, "Thank you for coming, Pam. I know it wasn't easy for you, but your being here has meant so much to Jeff, to all of us. I want you to know we appreciate it."

"But I haven't been able to do anything," Pam murmured, "to help at all."

A sad little smile curved Mrs. Moore's lips. "Just to have you here helped. The knowledge of friends around you, people who care—" she left it at that but the pressure of her fingers on Pam's tightened a little.

Later, when his mother had gone up to her room to lie down, Jeff suggested a walk. He told Pam, as they went out the back door of the farmhouse together, "I haven't had you to myself for a minute all day."

"I know," Pam said.

Then her hand was tight in Jeff's, exactly where it belonged and they were walking down a dusty path, past a red barn and the corner of the pasture, their steps matching, not saying anything. But understanding tempered their silence. Pam knew how Jeff felt and he knew she knew. Of what need were words between them?

They strolled through a little wood lot and in the shade there Jeff caught her close and kissed her as though he could never get enough of her lips, of the feel of her in his arms. And when his kiss was over, Pam told him, with no trace of uncertainty or doubt to make her words hesitant, "Jeff, I love you. I'm sure—so very sure."

He held her and laid his cheek against the dark softness of her hair. His voice was husky, asking, "How did you know I needed to hear that more than I ever needed anything before?"

"I needed to say it," Pam told him. "I've been getting more and more sure, Jeff—and now I know."

He sighed. "Things are in such a muddle, honey. I don't know how they'll work out, whether I'll have to take full charge here, or if I can go to school this fall."

"Of course, I hope you can," Pam told him. "But whatever happens won't matter, so long as we love each other—"

Jeff told her, "Dad knew, Pam. He was more sure of you than I dared let myself be. He liked you a lot and one of the last good talks we had together, he said to me, 'Don't worry, Jeff. Don't doubt. She'll make up her mind before long and it'll be all right. You'll see.' He sounded so confident."

"I'm glad," Pam said softly.

It was like being home, here in the sheltering circle of Jeff's arms. She felt safe and secure and so very certain this was where she belonged.

But they had to go back to the house before long. Pam was catching the seven o'clock bus and Jeff drove her to the station. She had said goodbye to his mother and the rest of the family. Now there remained only her good-bye to Jeff.

"I'll miss you more than ever now," she told him, waiting there in the crowded stuffy little bus terminal under the garish lights and advertising placards.

"Me, too," Jeff said. "But it won't be so long. I'll get up to see you one of these week ends. Maybe I'll know by then a little more about just where I'm at."

Pam knew where he was. Solidly planted in her heart.

All the way back to the town where the *Regina* was docked, Pam seemed to hear Jeff's final, whispered, "Just remember I love you," repeated over and over in her thoughts. The bus wheels said it and the stars seemed to spell it out against the gradually darkening sky. Now she knew how Penny felt, confident in the knowledge of Mike's love and of her love for him. It was wonderful to be sure at last. Even the uncertainty of Jeff's future plans didn't trouble Pam now. Things would work out for them somehow, sometime. She felt sure of it. . . .

112

Penny was delighted when Pam told her she'd made up her mind about Jeff. She hugged Pam and exclaimed, her eyes shining, "I'm so glad for both of you. Mike will be, too."

"Have you two been worrying about me?" Pam teased.

"A little," Penny admitted. "The way you were leading Alan on, just to make Geneva mad—well, it only seemed like a situation that could lead to trouble all the way around."

"Alan's fun," Pam said. "I like him as a friend. And Jeff wouldn't have any objection to our staying friends. But I won't lead him on any more, as you put it."

"If you don't," Penny said, "maybe Geneva will feel differently toward you."

"Maybe," Pam's smile was wry, "but I wouldn't count on it. And frankly, I don't care, so long as she leaves me alone."

One morning not long after Pam's return to the showboat, Alan came up to her as she was painting a flat on the deserted stage and inquired, "Am I imagining things, or have you been avoiding me lately?"

"Not exactly," Pam said, dipping her paintbrush in the can and continuing her job vigorously. "Let's just say I may not have been making myself quite as available as usual."

"Why?" Alan asked bluntly. "Is it anything I've done?"

Pam shook her head. "No, it isn't. I guess—it's just that I finally realized how much someone else means to me."

"Jeff Moore," Alan said thoughtfully. "Well, that figures. His father died, you went to the funeral, things got pretty emotional—"

"It wasn't just that," Pam broke in. "I've been trying to make up my mind about Jeff all summer and—now it's made up."

"He's the one, huh?" Alan grinned down at her.

Pam nodded.

"Okay." Alan continued to grin. "You've made that clear enough. I'm not going to try to break you and Jeff up. But is there any reason we can't associate with each other?"

"I guess not," Pam admitted, smiling, too. "Only, so long as Gen takes our friendship so hard, it seems—"

It was Alan's turn to interrupt. "I am getting," he said, "just a little sick of having all my relationships with other people cleared through Gen Day. If I tell her once and for all that we're through, can you and I continue to enjoy a quite harmless, casual friendship?"

An unhappy frown creased Pam's brow. "But I don't want you doing that on my account. I'd rather we just didn't date any more at all under the circumstances."

"I wouldn't," Alan told her. "But, of course, that's up to you."

The hint of hurt in his tone made Pam feel sorry. She said, "It's not that I don't like you, Alan. And we do have fun together. But Gen dislikes me so already, I think it's best if you and I just let things drop."

"You said you wouldn't let her push you around."

Pam smiled faintly. "Maybe my attitude toward her has been as childish as hers toward me. But that's no reason one of us can't start being sensible. And now that I'm sure how I feel about Jeff—"

"Do you have to keep rubbing that in?" Alan demanded.

"I'm sorry," Pam said. She turned back to her painting and, after a few silent minutes, Alan stalked off.

But Pam was mistaken in thinking that was the end of the matter. Soon the grapevine buzzed with the news that Alan had broken off with Geneva once and for all. Remembering his words on the subject, Pam couldn't help feeling a guilty qualm.

"But it wasn't my fault," she assured Penny. "I told him that wouldn't make any difference with us, that I didn't intend to date him any more whatever he did about Gen."

Penny's tone was troubled. "I suppose he just got tired of her hanging onto him, trying to order him around. You can't really blame him, and still—"

Pam admitted, "I feel sorry for her, too. I'm sure she was just putting up a bluff that day she told me she didn't care a thing about him."

"I hope," Penny said, "she doesn't figure you had any-thing to do with his telling her off."

"But she can't think that," Pam frowned and said, "if I don't date him, or pay much attention to him. . . ."

Still it proved rather difficult, she was to discover, to ignore someone who was bent and determined not to be ignored. Alan sought Pam out frequently, despite all she could do to discourage him. He tried to sit next to her at mealtime and took full advantage of those occasions when the work sheet threw them together on one job or another.

Finally Pam went to Mary Hatcher and specifically requested that she try not to assign them to the same job. "I hate to bother you about it," Pam told her, "but I'm honestly trying to avoid him."

Mary eyed her quizzically. "He's been on my neck to team you up as often as possible. Now I ask you! I ob-viously can't please you both!"

"Alan's being unreasonable," Pam told her. "I don't want Gen blaming me for their breakup."

"She'll be hard to convince, I'm afraid, unless Alan co-operates. Frankly," Mary went on, "I think the guy enjoys kicking up trouble. And he's so darned attractive, he can get away with murder. I know I have a hard time resisting him."

"Well, strengthen your will power," Pam coaxed, "and don't put us on any more jobs that take us off by our-selves."

"I'll try," Mary sighed, adding, "but it's hard enough uggling jobs around without getting personalities involved in the work sheet."

Not a very satisfactory conversation, Pam thought, as she headed back for the Hen Roost. Still, Mary would probably do what she could.

As Pam rounded a corner, her bare feet soundless on the sun-warmed boards of the deck, she came upon Gene-va, sitting and staring off into space. The other girl's face was turned away from Pam; she was unaware of her approach. There was a writing portfolio on her knees and a pen in her fingers.

Pam stopped and stood hesitant, moved by an urge to try once more to talk with Geneva. But the conviction grew in her that, if she made her presence known, the other girl would slam her portfolio shut with the insulting implication that Pam was seeking to intrude on her privacy.

And so she said no word, but instead backed away silently and took a different route to the Hen Roost.

CHAPTER SEVENTEEN

PENNY'S AND MIKE'S SURPRISE

TIP FLANDERS, COMFORTABLY limp on the battered chaise longue, remarked, "It's going to be sort of hard to adjust to regular classes after this summer."

"I know it," Pam agreed.

She was sitting cross-legged on the floor of the deck that opened off the Hen Roost. Penny perched on the rail nearby and several other girls were gathered around in attitudes of lazy relaxation. It was Sunday night, supper was over, and a good gab session seemed to be shaping up. The night all about was gray velvet trimmed in stars. Only the soft sound of the river and the querulous creaking of the old boat's timbers afforded a background for their young voices. This was a part of showboat life she would never forget, Pam thought. Sitting and talking, while the stars came out and a little breeze sprang up to dispel the day's heat and bring with it all the river's indefinable odors.

Penny murmured, "It just doesn't seem possible September's almost here."

"And yet," Pam said, "we seem to have been living on the showboat forever. It's hard to remember when we weren't."

Not that she'd found the summer dull. The days had passed too quickly, a bright montage of work and play, of parades and performances, of bidding good-bye to one

116

town and moving on upriver to another. But despite the busy days and nights, life on the *Regina* was geared to a slower tempo, a simpler routine than was customary nowadays either at home or college. It was a little as though they all had stepped backward in time for a while and now were going to have to make a conscious effort to catch up with the twentieth century again.

Penny's thoughts must have paralleled Pam's, for she said, a little note of amusement in her voice, "I'm even beginning to think like an old-timer. The idea of plenty of warm water and indirect lighting and sitting around watching television strikes me as sissy stuff."

"I know what you mean," Pam agreed. "But I expect we'll get used to modern conveniences fast enough."

Tip accused Penny, "You sound like Cap."

"Maybe I do," Penny admitted. "But some of his ideas make a lot of sense."

Carla Trent smiled crookedly. "I couldn't see that at first. I thought he was a complete old dodo. But now I find myself seeing things his way quite often. Do you suppose this summer's mellowed me?"

"It's mellowed us all a little," Tip said.

Practically all of us, Pam amended silently. She tried to brush the thought of Geneva aside, but it clung stubbornly, like a cobweb. Pam no longer dated Alan, she was no friendlier with him than any of the others. And the old rivalry between Geneva and her over the lead in the season's first play seemed long ago now and quite unimportant. How could Gen nurse a grudge so bitterly through the whole summer? But there was no use brooding over the impasse between them, so Pam pulled her thoughts determinedly back to the conversation.

Tip was saying, "If I evaluate all the good this summer's done me, I'd have to give myself an A for the course."

"Are you sure Buff would agree with your rating?" Carla laughed.

Tip shrugged. "I've had so much fun, I wouldn't mind a B or C."

"Do you suppose he'll flunk anyone?" Penny queried.

"I can think of one case where he should." There was a small drop of acid in Carla's voice. "After all, according to the catalogue, the showboat course is supposed to teach us to get along together." She left it at that, but there was no doubt in anyone's mind as to whom she meant.

Pam thought, I've tried to get along with Gen. I really want to. I hope Buff realizes that.

She believed he must. Buff was so quietly observant, he missed little that went on. But Pam was grateful that he continued to maintain a hands-off attitude. In nine cases out of ten such a course would work better than interference.

Only with Gen and her had he failed, Pam thought regretfully. But, after all, it took two to patch up a feud. . . .

Penny was walking ankle-deep in clouds these days, and for good reason. She and Mike, more to amuse themselves than for any serious purpose, had written a play. They called it *Love Triumphant* and it was a melodrama to end all melodramas.

As Mike put it, "Most of these old plays work up to one big climax, where the villain ties the heroine to the railroad track, or the hero gets himself trapped in the sawmill only a few inches from sudden death. But in our play there's a terrific climax in every act, almost in every scene! Boy, it's really hair-raising!"

Just for fun, they got a cast of special cronies together to read the various parts one lazy afternoon. The resultant hilarity could be heard all over the *Regina* and soon everybody aboard had assembled to listen, including Buff.

When Mike, who was supplying sound effects, yelled, "Final curtain! That's all!" there was a spontaneous outburst of applause.

Buff joined in wholeheartedly. "Maybe we've got us a couple of resident playwrights and don't know it," he chuckled. "The old touring companies used to do that, you know, carry their own writers along. I read somewhere that the playscript of *Uncle Tom's Cabin* was

118

written in just one week by a resident playwright, us
the novel as a basis, of course."

"Really?" Penny exclaimed, astonished. She was glow
ing with pride and pleasure over the reception her and
Mike's effort had received. And Mike, too, was beaming.

Buff nodded. He held out his hand for one of the
smudged scripts which the impromptu cast had been
sharing. "That sounded awfully funny to me—as much
of it as I heard. Do you mind if I read it?"

"Of course not," Mike exclaimed and Penny nodded
in quick agreement.

"If it's as good as I suspect," Buff grinned his slow
grin, "we just might put it on."

And that, to the surprise and delight of the flattered
co-authors, was exactly what he decided to do. Pam was
almost as thrilled at the prospect as Penny and Mike
were. And all the rest of the troupe got a charge out of
working on a play that had actually been written by
people they knew.

Even Geneva went out of her way to tell Penny, "I'm
glad for you. It couldn't have happened to anyone nicer."

Later, when Penny told Pam of Geneva's remark, she
added, "I tried to work the conversation around to you,
to sort of feel her out about why she can't let bygones
be bygones. But I might as well have tried to talk to
someone who was sealed away behind a sheet of glass
and couldn't even hear me."

"Thanks for trying, anyway," Pam said.

When she wrote to Jeff, she told him of the exciting
thing that had happened to Mike and Penny. "Their
play will open in Pittsburgh," she wrote, "and if you
could possibly get away and come for opening night, it
would be wonderful! They'd be so pleased—and I guess
you know how I'd feel about it."

Often her loneliness for Jeff ached in her with an actual physical pain. Not since his father's death had she
seen him. So many responsibilities, so much work, had
fallen on his shoulders, he'd been unable to get away.
Even his letters were hurried and unsatisfactory. Still,
Pam sensed in them a loneliness, a need that matched

own. This summer apart had made clear to both of ᵗhem that their feeling for each other was deep and true. ᵗt had been a period of growing up for Pam, of realizing values that had been vague and only half grasped at the summer's beginning. She knew now that she wanted to marry Jeff later on, whether the circumstances and setting for their life together would be what she would have chosen or not. When you loved someone, it wasn't important where you lived, so long he was there to help you adjust yourself to his background. Penny had known that from the beginning. Pam had taken a while to learn. But she was equally sure now and the knowledge gave her a sense of confidence and peace.

Jeff would be going back to college in the fall. Things had worked out for him in that respect. His sister and her husband had come to live on the farm and so Jeff could go on with his schooling. The awareness of this was like a beacon light, burning brightly ahead for Pam. For Jeff, too, she knew.

A faint smile curved her lips as she finished her letter. "I'll wait to see you until school starts if I have to but I won't like it! Do get to Pittsburgh if you can."

And she felt very sure Jeff would try. But she wasn't going to count on it and be disappointed.

The days that followed were busy ones, filled with rehearsals and preparations for the new production, as well as performances of the current play. There were sets to be altered and new ones devised, parts to learn, costumes to be made.

Penny and Pam were cast as orphaned sisters around whose tribulations the action of *Love Triumphant* revolved at a giddy pace. Geneva had the equally important role of their beautiful, but cruel stepmother. She plotted fiendishly with Alan, the villain, to rob them of their rightful inheritance under their wealthy father's will. The entire troupe threw itself into the production with marvelous enthusiasm, partly because everyone liked the play so well, and partly because of Penny's and Mike's general popularity. Even Geneva seemed willing to submerge her dislike of Pam in the joint effort to put on a really top-notch show.

"This is the sort of teamwork I like to see," Buff commended them all heartily. "You're shaking down into quite a bunch of troupers."

When the *Regina* docked at Pittsburgh one misty afternoon, it was her last stop of the season. Everyone turned out on deck for that final trip upriver and when the city sky line became visible Pam felt a little catch at her throat. She was sure the others felt it, too. The graceful birds, swooping low over the water, voicing their mournful cries, seemed to fit right into the mood of all the showboaters.

"Already I'm homesick for the *Regina*," Carla Trent admitted dolefully.

Pam nodded. She knew just what Carla meant. "We're still aboard, but for such a little time longer."

And Penny, standing beside Pam, murmured, "There'll never be another summer like this one. . . ."

Scarcely was the showboat settled in her new berth, the *Dink*'s motor stilled, the gangplank dropped, than Geneva hurried off on her customary trip to the post office. When she returned with the accumulation of mail that always awaited the *Regina* at a new stop, she made no attempt to disguise the fact that she had received more letters than anyone else. But Pam was too elated over Jeff's familiar black scrawl on an envelope to care.

She tore his letter open eagerly, her eyes raced along the lines. Then she looked up at Penny, face alight and mouth curving into a wide delighted smile.

"He's coming!" she announced. "Oh, Penny, I was afraid to count on it. But he's sure he can make it!"

"I'm glad!" Penny gave her a quick hug. "'I know how much you must want to see him."

"No, you don't," Pam denied good-humoredly. "Mike's right here where you want him. You've no idea how it's been, not seeing Jeff for weeks and weeks—but it's all right now."

Jeff was coming. The knowledge sang in Pam's heart

so loud and clear it was a wonder everyone couldn't hear it. He'd written that he'd be there Friday, the opening night of Penny's and Mike's play. That was only four days off. And anyone could live through four days, Pam reminded herself, especially such busy ones as these were bound to be.

But in spite of there being so much to do, time dragged for her. She did all the jobs assigned to her, she studied her lines for the new play and went through her small role in the current production each evening. She sewed on all her buttons and manicured her nails and still had time left over.

The final performance of the play they had been doing was on Wednesday night, giving them a free evening before *Love Triumphant* opened. Buff felt the break would do them good. The day was filled with rehearsals and work on props and costumes, but Pam knew the evening would be one of the longest she had ever lived through.

Penny and Mike planned to go into the city for dinner. They invited Pam to go along, but she declined, aware that they'd enjoy themselves more without a third party intruding.

Alan asked her to go into Pittsburgh with him. "We'll have dinner somewhere we can dance and see a floor show."

Pam smiled, shaking her head in the negative. "Thanks, Alan, but I'd rather not."

"Why?" he persisted. "You've been giving me the brush for days. A less persistent guy would have stopped trying long ago."

Pam suggested, "Why don't you take Geneva?"

But Alan said, "Oh, no! That's all wound up. I'd have a hole in my head to get it started again."

Pam was silent. It was really none of her business.

"Look," Alan coaxed in his most charming manner. "I know you're spoken for. I know Jeff Moore's it, so far as you're concerned. But is there any harm in being friendly?"

Pam smiled at him. "I'm friendly. I'm just not going to

122

date you. My heart wouldn't be in it. But any number of the other girls would be happy to go with you, I'm sure."

"Please," Alan said wryly, "don't bother building up my bruised and bleeding ego."

After supper the showboaters who had stayed aboard drifted up to the top deck. There were a dozen or so of them, including Alan, rather to Pam's surprise. Captain Anderson joined the sprawled figures in the deepening dusk and, urged on by a few leading questions, began spinning some of his entrancing tales of his life on the river. Other times and other ways seemed to grow real and distinct as he talked. The shifting, changing, colorful days of river-boating when the river had been the main stream of the nation's traffic, lacing the towns together at a time when the railroads were new and uncertain and airplanes undreamed of. The captain told of rough sights and vistas of sheer, untouched natural beauty, of deeds of bravery and cowardice. Shanty boats where people lived out their lives. Side-wheelers and stern-wheelers cutting through the water. Fleets of rafts, carrying logs, manned by rugged, singing timbermen. The river had been his life and his love. "And I'll be thankful if I can finish out my days on her," he told his intent audience. "I feel sorry for you kids, who only know enough about the old days to laugh at them and think they were queer and wild. In many ways we were more civilized then than now. There was time to enjoy life and live it at a reasonable pace. The world was at peace for a little while and it was good to be young and alive and know your future was in your own hands—" he broke off with a dry little chuckle. "There I go again. You shouldn't encourage me to talk about the past that's over and done with and that you can never know."

In the silence that followed his words, Alan began picking out lonesome sounding chords on his old guitar. And someone started singing and the others joined in. They sang the old songs they knew the captain liked best, and as their voices rolled out over the water in tribute to him, Pam knew this was one of the moments of the summer she would never forget, or ever want to.

CHAPTER EIGHTEEN

A SPECIAL OPENING NIGHT

FROM THE MOMENT the alarm clocks in the Hen Roost started sounding Friday morning practically no one aboard the *Regina* had any leisure time. Brushing her teeth over the rail beside Penny, Pam murmured, "How does it feel to be a playwright on the eve of your first production?"

"Even the butterflies in my tummy have butterflies," Penny admitted. "And Mike's just as bad. We went to a movie last night to try and forget about it and what did we do? Whispered about the play till everyone around us was so annoyed we had to move! And I haven't the vaguest idea what the picture was all about."

"Well, just simmer down," Pam advised, "or you'll never last through the day. It's a swell play and it will go over big, you'll see. People will probably be shouting for the authors when the curtain goes down."

"If they do I'll die," Penny gulped starkly.

All during the busy day, Pam's thoughts were more filled with Jeff than the play. She knew her part perfectly, rehearsals had been going well, all the troupe was convinced that *Love Triumphant* would have the audience roaring with laughter. So what was there to worry about? Every now and then Pam found herself caught up in the shining dream of Jeff's coming, a little smile curving her mouth, her hands arrested in the middle of whatever task she was about. If anyone spoke to her it took her a moment to get back to the immediacy of the present and try to grasp what was being said.

"Such daydreaming." Tip Flanders laughed at her once. "You're standing right here by me washing dishes and yet you're a million miles away."

Pam shook her head. "Not that far. Only about eighty-seven."

"I get it," Tip said. "And what are you and Jeff doing at this particular moment in your thoughts? Plowing the back forty, or feeding the pigs?"

"You're wasting your time trying to disillusion me," Pam told her. "I know life on a farm isn't the most glamorous in the world, but it's not half as bad as you think. Jeff's home is perfectly modern and quite attractive. There are some lovely antique pieces of furniture, an old cherrywood chest his mother's family brought across the plains in a covered wagon, a love seat with needlepoint cushions and—"

"I'll take modern any day," Tip put in. "Besides, you wouldn't want to live there with his mother, would you? That's the best way to wreck any marriage, according to the experts."

Pam said, "We haven't planned all the details yet, for pity's sake! We aren't figuring on getting married right away."

"That's good," Tip said frankly, "because I sure can't imagine you being a farmer's wife. And if you give yourself enough time to think about it, you'll probably change your mind."

Pam shook her head. "No, I won't. The way I feel about Jeff is for keeps. Just because I started out being fickle like you doesn't mean I can't grow out of it."

"Well, I like that," Tip objected good-naturedly. "I've been true to Cal all summer."

"A record for you," Pam said. "But what about when you get back to school and Bill Heath and Rick Colvin loom up in the picture again?"

Tip shrugged. " 'Variety is the spice of life,' to coin a phrase," she said, grinning. "I'll admit I'm not ready to settle down to one guy yet. But how can you be so sure you are? Look at the crush you had on Cade Venner only last winter."

The thought of Cade cast a small shadow in Pam's mind. Cade of the dark good looks, the moody unpredictable temperament. Cade who had wanted Pam to leave school and marry him and who had himself left Harwood when she refused. She hadn't heard of Cade or even thought of him in quite a long while. She was well over him and her feeling for Jeff made that brief infatuation seem like the feeble flicker of a candle in bright steady sunlight.

"Water over the dam," she told Tip.

"And you were sort of taken with Alan Richmond for a while," Tip argued. "Not that I blame you."

"That didn't mean anything," Pam denied. "Alan's fun and he is attractive, but with Jeff, it's different. It's sort of hard to explain, Tip, but I'm so sure about Jeff. There's such a warmth, a solidness, in our feeling for each other. It just doesn't leave any room for doubt. I've never felt like that about anyone before. He's so much more important to me than my own ideas about things. What I mean is— well, living on a farm, naturally that isn't exactly what I'd choose. But so long as that's Jeff's life and we'll be together, it'll be all right. I know that, because I'll do everything I can to help make it right. And we'll be happy, you'll see."

Tip stood for a moment, looking at her. "You really sound like you mean it," she said, a note of seriousness underlying her bantering tone. "In that case, I guess I'll have to give you my blessing after all."

The day raced on, filled to overflowing with all the things the day of an opening always was filled with. Hard work, leavened by heady excitement and thrilled anticipation. Buff seemed to be five places at once, supervising rehearsals, checking on sets and costumes, telling everyone to keep calm while he himself rapidly approached the boiling point. The Pittsburgh papers and radio stations had been generous with publicity. After all, a showboat was no common thing and they had built it up accordingly. Tickets were sold out for days ahead and all afternoon people kept coming down to the dock just to take a look at the *Regina*.

The showboaters felt themselves in a goldfish bowl of nonprivacy. But they were used to it by this time.

"It's going to seem sort of tame," Pam said to Penny, "to go back to shampooing your hair in the privacy of your bath."

She was stooped over a round granite pan on the sunny

deck off the Hen Roost, rinsing the lather out of her hair. Penny was pouring water over her twin's head from a big pitcher, borrowed from the galley. And from the shore several observers were watching the process with candid interest.

Penny, whose own newly washed tresses were tied up turban-fashion in a white towel, murmured an ambiguous "Ummmm." But when Pam lifted her head a moment later she saw by the slightly glazed look in Penny's eyes that she probably hadn't even heard what Pam said. Penny, between her responsibilities as co-author and actress, was in quite a dither.

"Hey!" Pam reached out to right the pitcher just before the wash pan ran over. "You can stop pouring now. I'm finished."

"Oh," Penny apologized, "I'm sorry. I didn't notice."

"Take it easy," Pam told her, "or you'll flip before tonight. Is Mike as excited as you are?"

Penny nodded, her smile gentle. "He's worse. He dreamed last night that everyone forgot his lines and the curtain wouldn't work and Buff said it was all Mike's fault because he thought up most of the play."

Pam laughed and hugged Penny, forgetting all about their interested audience on shore. "Do you suppose all playwrights suffer like you two over their first production?"

"If they do," Penny sighed, "I'm surprised anyone writes plays."

Dress rehearsal was held right after lunch. It went off almost without a hitch and Buff was well pleased. "This is going to be our best production yet," he assured the cast. "Now I want you all to do me a favor. Forget about the play till tonight and take it easy. Relax in any way you want to. Try to get as unkinked as possible. It'll do you good."

Relaxation took various forms for different people. Penny and Mike went for a long leisurely walk. Some of the girls lay down on their bunks to rest. The radio hams drifted to their transmitting station on the *Dink*. Others gathered on the upper deck, talking with Captain Anderson.

Pam, who had decided that her second-act costume looked rather mussed, carried the full-skirted dress up to the Hen Roost in order to press it. She set up the ironing board on the porch deck where it was fairly cool and went to work. When she had finished she hung the frock on a hanger and went inside to lie down. She closed her eyes, not sleeping, just thinking ahead to Jeff's visit and letting the deep pleasure of anticipation wash over her. But the warmth of the day was insidious and Pam was more tired from the rehearsal than she had realized. The next thing she knew she was being awakened from a sound sleep by Carla's hand on her shoulder.

And Carla was saying, "Boy, were you dead to the world! It's four o'clock and some of us are driving in to the Y to get a decent shower. Want to come along, or are you feeling rugged enough for the cold hose on deck?"

Pam yawned and stretched like a lazy kitten. "A real civilized shower sounds wonderful," she said. "Be with you in a second."

By the time the half dozen girls had gone into the city, had their showers at the YWCA and returned to the showboat, it was time for dinner. Between her excitement over the prospect of seeing Jeff, her mounting curiosity as to just when he would arrive and her regular first-night jitters, Pam found herself with little appetite.

She leaned across Mike, sitting beside her at the table, to ask Penny, "How are your butterflies now?"

"They're monsters," Penny admitted.

Even Mike, whose appetite was usually superb, wasn't in normal form tonight.

"Eat," Pam told him, "or you'll never have strength to shovel coal for the calliope."

"Cap hired a boy to take over for me tonight," Mike admitted, grinning. "He said it wasn't fitting for a budding dramatist to get all soot streaked on his first opening night."

"First?" Penny murmured faintly. "If you ever intend

to write another play, you'll have to get yourself another collaborator!"

"Let's wait and see how this one turns out before we make any rash decisions," Mike suggested, squeezing her hand.

When it was time for the concert, the *Regina* was bedecked and ready. Her banners fluttered crisply in the breeze. The soft-drink vending-machine was iced and waiting. The spotless auditorium had an expectant air and the box office was closed, with a NO MORE TICKETS AVAILABLE sign hung at the window. A little dusk breeze had come up as usual. With the first shrill notes of the calliope, people began to converge on the dock, as though drawn by invisible strings. Soon they would be coming aboard and finding their seats and the magic of the showboat would begin to take hold of them as it never failed to do.

In the cluttered dressing room backstage Pam was putting the finishing touches on her costume. She was dressing a bit early, not only to relieve the congestion, but also because she thought Jeff might put in an appearance any minute and she wanted to have a little time to talk with him before the show. It was almost half an hour till curtain time but surely he'd be here soon. She was adjusting her sash in front of the mirror when the realization struck her that she had left her second-act costume hanging on the porch deck outside the Hen Roost. She hadn't given it a thought since she had returned from the city, and evidently no one else had noticed it or thought to bring it down to the dressing room.

Pam told Penny, a faint frown of annoyance between her eyes, "I left one of my costumes upstairs when I ironed it. I'm all ready, so I'll get it now. Be back in a few minutes."

She left the dressing room and hurried along the deck toward the stairs, her hopeful glance skimming the crowd assembled on shore. But there was no sign of Jeff. The calliope music was almost deafening, but it had an exciting quality about it, Pam thought. Like the skirl of bagpipes. She hurried up the narrow stairway, her heel-less slippers quiet on the wood. Then just inside the door of the Hen Roost, she stopped abruptly.

Pam had fully expected to find it empty at this hour. She was startled to see Geneva Day, already in her ruffled net costume, standing at one of the dressers. Geneva's back was turned, but Pam could see her reflection plainly in the mirror. The other girl could have seen Pam, had she lifted her eyes to the glass. But she was bent over slightly and the rosy flickering glow of flame lighted her face. Pam's lips parted as she stared at Geneva, trying to see what she was doing.

The other girl was burning something that looked to Pam like a letter. She held it above an ash tray and the light from the flame gave her intent face an eerie unreality. Pam was appalled to see how close the fire licked to Geneva's flimsy voluminous costume.

The quick shocked intake of Pam's breath sounded loud at such close range. Geneva whirled around in surprise and, as she did so, the burning paper dropped from her fingers. A gasping scream escaped her as the wide flare of her skirt caught fire before Pam's horrified eyes.

CHAPTER NINETEEN

NEAR DISASTER

AFTERWARDS, THOSE NEXT nightmare seconds were never very clear in Pam's mind. She couldn't remember thinking at all. Terror caught at her as she watched greedy flames licking through sheer fabric, blazing higher about Geneva. For a shocked instant paralysis held Pam, then a purely involuntary reaction seemed to thrust her into movement. Something outside herself, something wiser and steadier, guided her groping hands to the blanket tossed providentially across the foot of a nearby bunk. Some voice, calm and sure, commanded from the depths of Pam's subconscious mind, "Wrap it around her! Smother the flames! Beat them out with your hands!"

And Pam obeyed the voice, shaken with fright though she was. She flung the blanket about Geneva, wrapping it tight with her own arms and body, beating desperately at the bright flames. And, in perhaps a minute at most, it was over.

There remained the sour stench of smoke, the smell of burned cloth, making Pam a little sick. Next the sharp stinging of her hands pricked her consciousness, and the sound of Geneva's hysterical voice moaning. "My leg, my leg—it's burned—it hurts!" She swayed, then collapsed in a heap on the floor, the blanket falling about her like a mantle.

Pam lifted the burned cloth from Geneva's knee. But her injury wasn't nearly so bad as Pam had feared. The stiffened petticoats under Geneva's costume had afforded considerable protection.

"You'll be all right." In her own ears Pam's voice sounded almost as unnatural as Geneva's, hoarse and rasping. And suddenly, now that danger was past, she felt anger rise in her. Sheer rage made her glare down at Geneva, demanding, "What on earth were you thinking of? Burning paper in here after all Cap's told us about what an awful hazard fire is on an old boat like this! Why, it could go up like kindling!"

Horror gripped Pam anew at the thought. But Geneva made no answer, only hunched there, rocking back and forth on the floor, sobbing, with tears running down her smudged cheeks. Pam reached out and picked up the half-burned letter that had been the cause of the accident. It wasn't really a letter at all, only an envelope addressed to Geneva and a blank sheet of paper. On the glass-topped dresser a little stack of blackened bits of paper and ashes indicated that Geneva had been at her strange task for some time.

Frowning, Pam went on, driven still by anger at the thought of the disaster the other girl's foolish action might have led to, "No letter's worth risking all our lives for.

131

And why do you imagine any of us would try to read your mail?"

Geneva's shoulders slumped forward. She buried her face in her hands. But she was no longer crying now. Tortured words began to pour from her as though a floodgate had been opened and she had no power to stop them, no hope of pretending any more. "Now you know," she choked. "Go on and tell the others! Somehow I always had the feeling it would be you who'd find out and give me away. Tell them—" her voice broke, then went on doggedly, despairingly, "that I wrote all the letters to myself. That's why I couldn't risk anyone seeing them. I tried to disguise my writing on the envelopes—but it wouldn't fool people really—not if they saw them close."

Pam could only stand there, staring down blankly at the other girl's bowed head, scarcely able to believe what she heard.

But before her lips could frame a question, or a word of denial, Geneva stumbled on, still in that dull, broken voice that brought a lump of aching pity to Pam's throat. "You wouldn't know how it feels never to get any mail when everyone else does. Your family's not too busy for you. Your mother and father—why, they came all the way out here just to see you. And he's only your stepfather, too."

Geneva laughed then, a grating terrible sound. She lifted her head to look up at Pam and her mouth twisted bitterly. "You want to know all about stepfathers? Just ask me, I'm an expert on them. I've had three and I doubt some of them even remember my name. Not one of them cares a darn about me, or what happens to me. Why should they when my own mother doesn't?"

The tortured voice went on and Pam listened, torn between shock and pity. Geneva's mother was beautiful and glamorous, she hadn't lied about that. But Elissa Day shrugged off her motherhood lightly. She preferred her friends to forget about Geneva. It made her seem less young to have a daughter almost through college. And Geneva's father had remarried, she hadn't even heard from him in years.

"Do you blame me," she asked, "for making up a more satisfactory set of parents to impress people with? They never even write—all they do is send me money. And when I'm home, half the time no one else is there. Oh, I could stay if I wanted to, but just with a bunch of servants." She sighed, a deep heart-touching sound. "You might as well know the whole story. I'm sick of trying to hide it all. The only reason Buff let me take the show-boat course was because I begged him so. I told him the truth, that I had absolutely no place else to go except to stay alone in our Santa Monica house or go rattling around some resort by myself." A faint smile curved her mouth. "Buff's a good joe, though. He wouldn't give me away. So I made trouble for him by coming late and squabbling with you and some of the others. Sometimes," she frowned, "I don't know what gets into me. It's—as if I have to be mean and arrogant to people, just so they can't guess how awful and—terribly alone I feel inside. I have to put up a big front, lie about how crazy my parents are over me, pretend—" her voice died and she drew a deep breath and straightened her shoulders a little. "But there's no use pretending any longer. Now you know all there is to know about me."

Tears stung at Pam's eyelids. She had never felt so sorry, so wholeheartedly, unreservedly sorry for anyone in her life as she felt for Geneva at this moment. With all defenses down, her arrogance in ruins, she was completely broken and pitiful. Pam's eyes moved from her uplifted face to the scorched remains of the letter still clasped in her own fingers. And a mighty resolve rose in her, an instinct of protection so strong that she could not have resisted it had she been moved to try.

Pam's voice was low, but fierce with determination. "Now you listen to me! Don't tell anyone else a thing about this, about the letters. I won't have it! No one knows what you've done but you and me. And I won't tell a soul. I give you my word!"

"But—" aquamarine eyes widened in surprise, "why should you cover up for me?"

"What do you think I am?" Pam demanded. She was

133

busy now, gathering up the telltale scraps of scorched paper and ashes, adding them to the half-burned letter she still held. She wadded the whole mess into her handkerchief and stuffed it deep down in the waste basket, under a protective layer of cleansing tissues and discarded boxes and paper. "No one will find it there. And we won't tell anyone what you were doing, either of us. You'd be in a bad jam if Buff and the captain knew you were deliberately burning anything here in the Hen Roost. But an accident—that could happen to anyone." She thought for a moment, frowning, then went on firmly, "You were lighting a cigarette and the match backfired when you struck it and your costume caught on fire. That sounds plausible enough to fool anyone. I was just coming in and helped you put it out. If we both stick to that story, no one will know the difference. And we'll both stick to it."

Geneva murmured, her voice only a breath above a whisper, "You won't tell—you mean it?"

"Of course!" Pam stooped and gently helped the other girl to her feet. At the contact it was as though some current passed between them, of warmth and friendliness and confidence.

How little anyone ever knows another, Pam thought, until some crisis, physical or emotional, gives them the gift of understanding.

She and Geneva might have gone on forever, shut away from each other, their vision warped by the surface clash of personalities. And yet, when the curtain was pulled aside by something beyond them both, it was as though they saw each other clearly for the first time, and their preconceived prejudice and dislike dropped away.

Poor kid, Pam found herself thinking. No wonder she invented a kind of dream world to keep us all from finding out the truth. And then she had to continue embroidering it and adding new details to keep it all from tumbling down around her. That's why she wouldn't let anyone get too close, for fear they'd see through her and sense the truth. Penny realized that partly, but neither of us understood why. It was fear that made Gen seem so

134

possessive and dominating toward Alan till she finally lost him. Fear that he'd not want her any more and she'd be left more alone than ever. But Alan's no good for her. She's better off without him. Maybe I can help her see that, but later.

Under her hands, Pam felt the other girl straighten, as though new strength were coursing through her. Gen said, "I can never thank you enough. I'm—so ashamed of the way I've treated you—and then to have you save my life—" her voice broke.

"I've been pretty stinky to you, too," Pam said, a slight smile twisting her lips. "And you'd have helped me, I'm sure, if it had been the other way round."

Gen shook her head. "I'd have got panicky, just as I did when this happened. I—I'd have wanted to help, but— I might not have had the courage. You saved the lives of all the others, too. If the boat had caught fire—"

"Don't think about it," Pam interrupted. "It's over now." She asked then, "Do you think your leg's burned too badly to go on with the show? Shall I have someone call a doctor?"

Geneva shook her head, her eyes luminous. "It isn't bad. I can manage if we put some salve and a sort of bandage on it, so my dress won't brush against it. But—" she broke off and her glance dropped, appalled, to the ruin of her costume, "I can't go downstairs and across the boat like this. Everyone will see me—all the people who've come aboard for the show!"

Pam hurried toward the porch deck. "Must have been fate made me leave this costume up here earlier." She was back in a second, the dress she wouldn't need till the second act held in her hands. "We'll have to tell the rest of the troupe and Mrs. Marley. She's got all the first-aid stuff. But the audience needn't know a thing, if we hurry—" She broke off at the sound of rapid footsteps approaching the Hen Roost. "Wash your face quickly," she whispered to Geneva, "and fix your hair. I'll help you dress."

A look passed between them, of confidence on Geneva's part, of assurance on Pam's. Then Penny burst in, demanding, "Pam, what on earth's taking you so long? It's almost—" she stopped with an appalled gasp at sight of Geneva. "What happened?"

"An accident," Pam said. "Come on, Penny. If we both help, she'll be ready sooner. She was lighting a cigarette and the match sort of exploded and caught her on fire."

If she could convince Penny, who knew her so well, Pam thought, she could be persuasive enough to convince anyone that she was telling the truth. And certainly a lie that hurt no one and helped someone so much was justified.

"How awful!" Penny exclaimed, her eyes wide with sympathy as she moved to assist Geneva. "But if she's badly hurt—"

"I'm all right," Geneva said staunchly. "Don't worry."

"But—you're burned, too!" Penny stared at Pam's reddened palms.

"A little," Pam had to admit. Her hands stung, but the emotional impact of the scene with Geneva had driven all thought of her own discomfort from her mind. "I'll have Mrs. Marley put some salve on them when she bandages Gen's knee. And my lace mitts will cover them up, so the audience won't notice."

Geneva had managed to remove most of the damage to her make-up caused by her tears and the smoky smudge. Now Pam and Penny helped her slip from one costume into the other.

As she brushed her hair hastily, Geneva said, her eyes shining, "I look practically as good as new."

"Better," Pam told her, "to me, at least."

Penny could only stand there, staring blankly, as Pam's arm went around Geneva in a heartening, encouraging hug.

CHAPTER TWENTY

THE SHOW GOES ON

MRS. MARLEY, hastily summoned by Penny to administer first aid for Gen's burned leg and Pam's slightly scorched hands, clucked sympathetically over them both.

"You poor dears!" the kindly housemother exclaimed, shaking her white head as she went competently to work with ointment and gauze dressings. "You might have been dreadfully burned! And I shudder to think of what could have happened if the fire had spread. All these people aboard, and the boat so old—there might have been a terrible panic!"

"Don't think about it," Pam told her. "It didn't spread. And we're not even going to let the audience know anything happened, unless—" she turned her solicitous glance toward Gen, "your knee's too painful for you to go on?"

"No, it'll be all right," Gen insisted. "The salve and the dressing's already beginning to help. I don't want it to ruin the show—Penny's and Mike's show. I won't let it!"

Penny pressed her hand gratefully. "You're very brave," she murmured. "And you, too, Pam. I don't know how to thank you both."

"Skip it," Pam said with a little grin. "But you'd better hurry and tell Buff we're coming. He'll be having fits!"

The steady look that passed between Pam and Gen made the housemother's observant eyes widen in wonder. Nor was the change in their attitude toward each other lost on the rest of the troupe when the two girls arrived backstage.

Penny had already told Buff and the cast what had happened, or what she had been led to believe had happened. So Geneva and Pam were at once the center of a sympathetic crowd. Everyone exclaimed over Gen's courage in going on in her part, despite her injury. And Pam, to her surprised embarrassment, found herself being hailed as a heroine. All the cast hovered around, asking questions and commending Pam for her clearheadedness and bravery. As for her insistence that she had done no more than any of them would have, under like circumstances, she might as well have saved her breath. Especially when Geneva told them all, her glance appreciative on Pam's face, "If she hadn't happened along when she did, the whole boat could have caught fire!"

Buff was sympathetic, but he warned them all against letting word of the near disaster spread to the audience. "People get panicky," he said, "and, after all, the danger's past now. There's no use causing a sensation. If you're both sure you can go on, we'll ring up the curtain." At the two girls' nods of agreement, he said, "Places, everybody. We're already late."

Pam smiled at Geneva, and said, "Good luck!"

"To you, too," Gen murmured. And her answering smile was aloof no longer, but warm and wide.

As Gen moved across the stage, out of earshot, Carla Trent whispered to Pam, "Well, glory be! It looks like peace has been declared at last!"

And Tip Flanders added, "Well, wouldn't you feel a little kindlier toward someone who had just saved your life?"

"Don't," Pam heard herself rising to Gen's defense. "She's had a rough time. Let's all help her as much as we can."

She realized Tip and Carla would assume she meant they should help Gen get through the performance. But her words had a farther-reaching significance than that. There was no wall shutting her away from Gen now, holding the other girl a prisoner in a world of her own imagining. Pam felt close to Gen, closer than anyone had ever been permitted to come, for fear they might see through Gen's pathetic pretenses. Pam knew the whole truth about her and the fact that she was determined to keep Gen's secret seemed to tie them together with a strong bond of understanding. They were friends now, who had been enemies. And Pam felt sure the desire to go on being friends was as real in Gen as it was in her.

138

Tip murmured in an awed tone, "I think you're terrific. I'd have just stood there—I know it! My reflexes don't reflex in an emergency. They get paralyzed."

"Don't be silly," Pam argued. "You'd have grabbed the nearest blanket, too. That's all I did, without even thinking."

Carla shook her dark head admiringly. "You really have to give Gen credit, too. Look at her out there—her leg must be hurting like fury, but you'd never guess it from her performance. What a trouper!"

"Isn't she, though?" Pam nodded. "I'm proud of her."

She heard her own cue then and moved out onto the stage, speaking her lines without hesitation. And the magic of acting caught her up, just as it always did. The glow of the lights, the sense of people's faces in the dimness beyond the rim of the stage, pushed all thought of her own identity aside. She proceeded to lose herself in the part she was playing, just as all the others were losing themselves, were becoming for a time the characters Mike and Penny had created.

A board of the old stage creaked slightly for no apparent reason. And Pam wondered whimsically if the *Regina* might not be haunted by the gentle ghosts of other players, who had gestured and said their lines in other plays during all the years of the showboat's colorful existence. All troupers together, Pam thought, past and present, bound to each other by the unchanging creed of the theater—the show must go on.

And this particular show was going on very well, despite all that had happened. The players threw themselves into it with fine fervor and the audience responded with more than the customary amount of applause, of good-natured booing and hissing. Or did she imagine that, Pam wondered, because this was Penny's and Mike's play and she felt so proud of them? She didn't really think her judgment was prejudiced, though. Buff had predicted this would be their best production and it seemed he was right.

It was toward the end of the first act that Pam glanced out across the footlights and saw Jeff's familiar face looking intently up at her from his aisle seat near the front. Her heart spilled over with quiet happiness. The only thing that stopped her from giving him a warm smile was the extremely tragic tempo of the scene she was playing. The audience might be a bit mystified if a girl who was just about to be enticed to her doom by a dastardly villain suddenly started beaming. But Jeff was there, not more than twenty feet away from her. And as soon as the play was over— But she mustn't think of that now, or she'd surely forget her lines.

When the final curtain was drawn and the continuing applause had summoned the cast back for several calls, Buff stepped out onto the stage and lifted his hand for quiet.

His pleasantly homely face below the bristling crew cut was beaming. He announced, motioning toward the wings, "We have the two authors of this original play right here on the showboat. Would you like to meet them?"

The audience indicated unmistakably that it would like nothing better. And when Penny, still in costume, and Mike, actually blushing a little, came out on the stage hand in hand, the roar of applause heightened till it seemed the *Regina*'s ancient auditorium could scarcely contain it.

"Speech! Speech!" someone called out and others took up the chant.

Mike, for all his usual assurance, could do no more than gulp a few stumbling words of thanks. And Penny just shook her head and smiled her gratitude tremulously. But their modesty seemed to endear them to the crowd more than eloquence. And the clapping and whistling swelled again. At last, though, the curtains met with an air of finality and stayed closed. And people began to drift out in leisurely manner, talking and laughing.

Pam couldn't shut out the thought of how different the scene might have been if that small fire in the Hen Roost had spread. Panic and tragedy could have resulted, turning this night of Penny's and Mike's happy triumph into a nightmare of disaster.

She became aware of Geneva, standing close beside her in the wings. For a moment neither of them spoke, but the new depth of understanding between them made Pam almost sure that the other girl's thoughts were similar to her own.

And then Gen asked, smiling at Pam, her eyes luminous, "Do you ever wonder about things like—fate? I mean, whether there's some pattern in the way things happen?"

"Sometimes, a little," Pam admitted.

And Geneva went on, "If you hadn't just happened to come to the Hen Roost at the moment you did—" she left it at that.

"But if I hadn't come," Pam reminded, "your dress might not have caught fire at all. I startled you, without meaning to, of course."

"I'm glad you came, though." Geneva's voice was low, earnest. "We would never have reached this point if something hadn't happened to make me realize I could trust you."

"You can trust lots of people," Pam told her, "if you'll let them come close enough to know you, to become friends, as we're friends now."

Geneva's face lit up. "I'll try, Pam. Really, I will."

"That's all it takes," Pam told her.

Penny and Mike came up to them then, and there was no further chance for private conversation. But all the things had been said, Pam thought, that needed saying at this moment. Time would take care of the rest. And friendship, real friendship, took time. But they had made a start tonight, she and Geneva. They had seen each other, in a second of revelation, whole and true and without pretense. And each had liked what she saw and would make of it a foundation to build on for the future. . . .

Pam didn't stop in the dressing room to change her costume. Now that the play was over, Jeff took full possession of her thoughts. She couldn't get to him quickly enough. Hurrying out the little side door from backstage, she glimpsed a tall familiar figure waiting there on the narrow deck.

"Jeff—oh, Jeff—" his name was a whisper on her lips. Then she was in his arms, feeling their muscular strength about her. And there was no need for words, no need at all. Their kiss said everything that must be said between them. It told of their loneliness for each other that was over now, of their need that was greater than it had ever been. It was the kiss of a man and a woman who loved each other, in whose hearts there wasn't room for doubt. No longer was Pam unsure as she had been at the summer's beginning. And these months apart had strengthened Jeff's certainty that this was the girl he wanted for his wife.

"Pam," his voice was husky with feeling when he finally spoke, "I've missed you so!"

But Pam had known that from the hunger of his kiss. She whispered shakily, "Me, too." And then she told him, "I've grown up this summer, Jeff. I'm sure, so very sure, I love you."

But her lips hard against his had told him that.

"I love you," Jeff murmured, his breath stirring the soft hair at her temple. "I always have. But I wanted you to have this summer."

Pam nodded. She had had her summer and she was grateful, for it had taught her much. The sunny months of work and play had brought heartaches and triumphs, misunderstanding and the promise of a rich friendship that was only just beginning. From Buff and the others she had learned the joy of working together as a team, of submerging her own personality when that was necessary for the good of the joint effort. From old Captain Anderson she had absorbed an appreciation of the past, with its different ways and slower tempo.

Pam thought wonderingly, I'm really not the same girl who stepped aboard the *Regina* in June. All of us have changed some, matured a little, broadened our outlook,

142

had a few of the sharp edges of conceit and intolerance smoothed down.

The doubt that had troubled her then, as to whether she had within her the capability of being a good wife for Jeff, had been dissipated. She was sure now and with that surety had come the most wonderful sense of confidence in the future that Pam had ever known.

"We're going to be all right," she told Jeff.

"I know it," he said, and his voice sounded as sure as hers.

The old timbers of the *Regina* creaked peacefully and the moonlight fell on Pam's face and glinted in her eyes as she lifted her lips to Jeff's. Somewhere on the boat Alan began picking out a tune on his ancient guitar and clear young voices rose in song. "I love you truly, truly, dear," rolled out across the water.

It seemed to both Pam and Jeff that the choice of a song couldn't have been more appropriate.

THE END

Other titles you will want to read—all at 40¢.
See below for our SPECIAL offer.

Y855   VAGABOND SUMMER   Anne Emery
Peg Madison goes on a hosteling trip, sees the country, and
finds a purpose in life.

Y845   BEANY AND THE BECKONING ROAD
                                        Lenora Weber
Beany gets her chance to travel, and further complicates her
already complicated life.

Y841   TRISH   Margaret Maze Craig
Patricia Ingram comes up against some very serious problems
when she falls in love with the most sophisticated boy in
school.

Y839   BECKY'S ISLAND   Elisabeth Ogilvie
Vicky Conrad has to land on Becky's Island, and this simple
act changes her entire life.

Y838   ALONG COMES SPRING   Mildred Lawrence
Talented Cory Carmichael's grim determination to do well in
college nearly spoils her freshman year.

Y827   WHERE IS MY HEART?   Amelia Walden
When Carol Turner starts practice teaching, she finds herself
ill-prepared for the job, and many problems develop.

Y818   PASSPORT TO ROMANCE   Betty Cavanna
Fifteen-year-old Jody Scott spends a thrilling year at a school
in Switzerland.

These books are available at your local newsstand or

ORDER ANY FIVE FOR $2.00
POSTAGE FREE!

On single copy orders send 40¢ plus 10¢ for postage
and handling to BERKLEY PUBLISHING CORPORA-
TION, 15 E. 26th Street, New York, New York 10010.

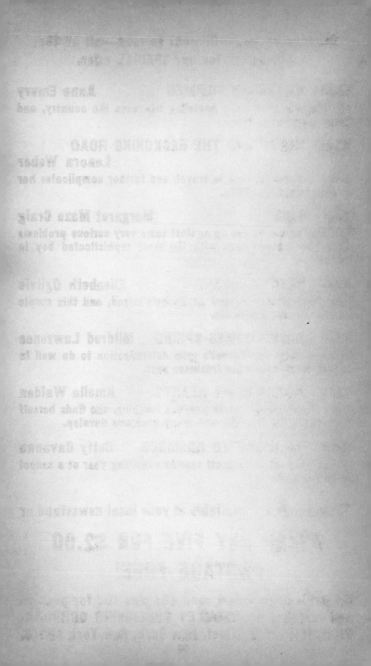